"What are you doing?" Jessie demanded.

The gunshot exploding through the air answered her question for him.

She would have screamed if Henry hadn't clamped his hand over her mouth. He had his entire body wrapped around her, pressed against the rock.

But someone had shot a gun. At them. Oh God.

"Don't start panicking, Jessie. Okay? We're not going to panic."

It was an order, and it kept her tethered to this moment. No panicking. No letting her brain tumble into the possibilities. They weren't shot, and Henry was here with his military background. They were all right. They would be all right.

She wouldn't think about all the Sarabeth what-ifs. She couldn't. She could only focus on...on...

"Take a deep breath," Henry said low in her ear. "Count to three. Then let it out. Same count. You hear me?" She nodded and he took his hand off her mouth.

"Why would anyone shoot at us?" she asked, her voice sounding shaken.

"No idea. But we're going to find out."

SHOT IN THE DARK

Nicole Helm

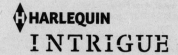

To good moms and dads of all types.

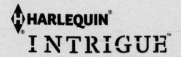

INTRIGUE™

ISBN-13: 978-1-335-58254-6

Shot in the Dark

Copyright © 2023 by Nicole Helm

Recycling programs
for this product may
not exist in your area.

For questions and comments about the quality of this book,
please contact us at CustomerService@Harlequin.com.

Harlequin Enterprises ULC
22 Adelaide St. West, 41st Floor
Toronto, Ontario M5H 4E3, Canada
w.Harlequin.com

ed in U.S.A.

Nicole Helm grew up with her nose in a book and the dream of one day becoming a writer. Luckily, after a few failed career choices, she gets to follow that dream—writing down-to-earth contemporary romance and romantic suspense. From farmers to cowboys, Midwest to *the* West, Nicole writes stories about people finding themselves and finding love in the process. She lives in Missouri with her husband and two sons, and dreams of someday owning a barn.

Books by Nicole Helm

Harlequin Intrigue

Covert Cowboy Soldiers

The Lost Hart Triplet
Small Town Vanishing
One Night Standoff
Shot in the Dark

A North Star Novel Series

Summer Stalker
Shot Through the Heart
Mountainside Murder
Cowboy in the Crosshairs
Dodging Bullets in Blue Valley
Undercover Rescue

A Badlands Cops Novel

South Dakota Showdown
Covert Complication
Backcountry Escape
Isolated Threat
Badlands Beware
Close Range Christmas

Visit the Author Profile page at Harlequin.com.

CAST OF CHARACTERS

Henry Thompson—Former military man and current rancher who is drawn into helping a single mom and her daughter as danger surrounds them.

Jessie Peterson—Single mom, desperate to protect her child from her dangerous family and wants to put roots down in Wilde, Wyoming, where she spent her childhood.

Sarabeth Peterson—Eleven years old, headstrong and desperate to protect her mother from a secret she has. Wants Henry to help protect them and will run away to get him to do it.

Rob Currington—Sarabeth's father—Jessie ran away from him before Sarabeth was born.

Landon Thompson—One of Henry's brothers who Sarabeth saved from her father a month ago. Also former military and current rancher. Computer expert.

Cal, Dunne, Brody and Jake—The remaining Thompson brothers, who all ranch together. Had to take on new lives after a terrorist group unearthed their real identities back when they were in the military as a secret ops team that took down terrorist targets.

Hazeleigh and Zara Hart, and Kate Phillips—The brothers' significant others, who also live on the Thompson property and help Jessie and Sarabeth when they come to the brothers for help.

Chapter One

Sarabeth Peterson was eleven years old. She had done a lot in her short life. Moved from Florida to Arizona and then to Wyoming. She'd helped protect her mother from all the varying family who wanted to hurt her.

And then, a month ago, she'd killed her father.

Self-defense, of course. And she hadn't really known him anyway. Mom had kept her as far away from Rob Currington as she could, but he'd found them last month. Hurt Mom. Used her.

And Sarabeth had shot him. Saved them.

But she knew they weren't safe yet. Mom thought the fact the old bank robbery gold had been found meant people would stop looking.

Sarabeth knew better. There was more—so much more—and someone was going to figure out she was the one who knew about it.

Luckily, there was someone who could help her.

The problem was finding a way to talk to Henry Thompson without her mother finding out. Mom would find a way to talk Henry out of helping them. Sarabeth had to keep it a secret. Usually not easy to do, but Mom had been busy the past month—talking to the police, and family services, and getting a job at a company that offered people stagecoach rides so they could pretend they were back in the old days or something.

Adults were weird.

But they were staying in Wilde, Wyoming. Sarabeth was happy about that. She liked it here. Better than Florida and Arizona. She liked the mountains and the ranches and all the *space*. It was like an adventure.

Adventures were fun, but they were also dangerous. They were going to need some help. They were going to need some protection.

A phone call wouldn't work—she wasn't sure anyone would listen to her over the phone. Mom didn't let her use the computer without supervision, so email wasn't on the table.

It had to be done face-to-face.

"Sarabeth."

She had to turn her attention away from her plans to the man she didn't trust sitting in front of her. She liked the lady from family services. Maybe she didn't always agree with Ms. Angie, but the social worker had a nice smile. And she didn't talk to Sarabeth like she was a dumb little kid.

The family counselor, Dr. Evan, was another story. And she didn't like his eyes. Flat and brown and too... something. She didn't like the way he looked at her. It made her angry.

Sarabeth was used to being angry, but she usually understood why. She didn't know why Dr. Evan made her angry, only that he did. And Mom had always said to listen to her gut feelings. When you didn't, you ended up tied up in a basement.

At least, that was what had happened to Mom. After ten years of keeping them away from Sarabeth's dad, Mom's luck ran out and Rob had showed up at exactly the wrong moment and brought them to Wyoming against Mom's will.

Sarabeth hadn't liked her father, but she *had* liked trying to find the gold. She'd hated that Rob had hit and hurt her mother, but Sarabeth had done something about it. Hadn't she?

"What are you thinking about?"

She fingered the piece of gold in her pocket. It had been her dad's. Well, technically, he had stolen it from a man who was maybe *his* dad, but dead now. Because of her father.

Who was dead now, because of her.

That was kind of weird, wasn't it? It was a thought she would have shared with Ms. Angie. She wasn't about to share it with Dr. Evan.

"I don't like it when my mom's not in here," Sarabeth said. She didn't scowl at Dr. Evan, even though she wanted to. Because sometimes you had to pretend to get what you wanted. And she wanted to not have to come to these dumb appointments anymore.

Dr. Evan's face changed. It got kind of pinched like he was irritated with her, but his smile stayed put and his words weren't mean.

"We thought maybe you'd feel more comfortable talking about your father without her in the room."

"I'm not," Sarabeth returned flatly. She didn't want to discuss anything with Dr. Evan, but especially her father.

"All right."

Sarabeth didn't believe his smile for a second, but he pushed a button on his phone and asked somebody to send Mom in.

"I think we've got about as far as we can today," Dr. Evan said to Mom. "We'll see you at your appointment next week, Sarabeth."

"Thank you, Dr. Young." Mom put her arm around Sarabeth and started leading her to the door.

Sarabeth knew she shouldn't. Mom told her to be nice and polite to people who wanted to help, but Sarabeth couldn't always resist poking at somebody. Especially a somebody she just didn't like.

"Bye, Mr. Evan." He *hated* when people called him Mr. instead of Dr. She'd found that in her first appointment with him.

She'd said it once every appointment since.

His nice smile fell and Sarabeth had to hide her grin behind her hands as Mom led her outside.

"That was wrong, Sarabeth," Mom muttered as they waved at the front desk lady and then left.

"I'm sorry, but I don't like him. You said I don't have to talk to people I don't like." Sarabeth squinted at the summer sun as she looked up and down the street.

Wilde was by far the smallest town they'd ever lived in. There wasn't even a grocery store here. It was a strange place, but that was what Sarabeth liked about it. It felt odd and out of place like she did.

Still, she preferred the ranches out past town. All that

land. Horses. Big sky and space. Sarabeth felt alive and in control out there. But town was okay too.

One of the Bent County stagecoaches went by and Mom waved at the driver. They started walking down the road. They lived in an apartment above a hardware store just down the block. Mom had lived there when she was a little kid with her grandma.

Before they got very far, Sarabeth saw a familiar silver truck. She looked wildly around for any of the Thompson brothers, hoping for one in particular to materialize. But wherever they were, they weren't in or around their truck.

That truck would eventually go back to the Thompson ranch, where Henry was—if he wasn't the one driving it. Sarabeth slowed her pace and pulled her hand out of Mom's grasp.

"Jessie!" someone called. Mom tensed, but she plastered on a smile. Sarabeth knew Mom couldn't stand nosy Mrs. Caruthers who ran the hardware store with her husband, but Mrs. Caruthers had not picked up on it.

"What have you two been up to?" Mrs. Caruthers asked, smiling her big, toothy smile. Her eyes were beady though. And always watching.

Sarabeth shifted to stand behind mom. "Hello, Mrs. Caruthers," Mom greeted. "How are you today?"

Mom was good at that. Not answering questions. They'd spent a lot of time hiding, lying, *not* answering questions that might make her father or Mom's family come after them.

Mrs. Caruthers was talking about some foot problem she had, but Sarabeth wasn't listening. She was looking at the silver truck. She knew it was one of the Thompson brothers'. *Knew* it.

Her lucky gold piece was giving her the chance. She let go of Mom's hand. "Mom, can I go buy a piece of candy?"

Mom looked down at her, eyebrows drawn together. She looked into the store window they were standing in front of, then sighed and gave a little nod.

But Sarabeth didn't go into the store. She backed slowly away, toward the truck, watching Mrs. Caruthers's mouth move and move and move.

Sarabeth scrambled up into the truck bed as quiet as a mouse. She curled herself into a little ball in the corner and waited, hoping against hope the Thompson brother would return soon and drive off. Before Mom realized she wasn't coming back.

She didn't think of how worried Mom would be or how much trouble she'd be in. She just thought about how she could finally get the help Mom needed.

HENRY ROYAL HAD been more than happy to leave his last name behind when his superior officer had informed him of the military leak that necessitated he and his team members be killed on paper, then sent to the middle of nowhere, Wyoming, to ranch with a new last name.

Royal held nothing but tragedy and bad memories attached. Thompson was like a new start.

He wished the new start included a little less cow waste, and really wished it included a lot less of his military brothers bringing *women* into their lives. Zara had been fine enough. A ranch woman, always ready and willing to go toe to toe with his bad temper and scathing sarcasm, and Jake was happy so that was that.

Kate, on the other hand, was a softer sort, and Henry didn't care for *soft* even if Brody did. And if Kate was soft, Hazeleigh was downright pillow fluff, the opposite of her sister Zara. But Landon was dedicated to the sweet woman.

All their love bull gave Henry an itch between his shoulder blades. Only bad things could come of *love* and committing your life to each other. He'd learned that lesson early and not a damn thing in his life had ever changed his mind.

Jake didn't agree as he and Zara were now engaged. No doubt Brody and Landon would fall into the same trap soon enough.

Luckily, his other two brothers were as likely to form romantic attachments as Henry was to sprout wings. Taciturn, injured Dunne. Stick-up-his-ass former commander Cal.

No, the three of them were safe. Thank God.

Henry parked the truck in front of the big house that now felt too dang crowded. Though Landon and Hazeleigh had moved into the cabin across the yard, Henry had still been conned into the big house, agreeing to give Brody and Kate the little shack outbuilding he'd redone into a nice room.

Henry still complained bitterly about it, though Kate being an amazing cook made it worth the while. Zara took a turn washing dishes—which was one less turn he had to take. It wasn't all bad.

Not that he'd let anyone know that.

Henry preferred to focus on the bad. That way when it came and bit you on the ass, you were ready.

He slammed his truck door, headed for the house, but then he heard a strange…sound. He looked back at the truck, and there was a little girl.

The little girl they'd helped last month. "What are you doing here?" he demanded, taking in her wind-blown brown hair and red-cheeked face.

"I need your help," she said, hopping out of the truck with a child's ease.

He looked in the bed of the truck, trying to figure out where the hell she came from. "You didn't ride in there all the way from town, did you?"

"I absolutely did."

He was losing his touch. That was concerning. There'd been a day he wouldn't have driven an inch without knowing, instinctively, there was a stowaway in his truck.

Of course, he wasn't used to stowaways asking for help rather than wanting to kill him.

She fisted her hands on her hips and looked up at him. She was fierce, he'd give her that. But she was a tiny thing—far too skinny for her frame, all angles and vinegar.

He'd been impressed by her vinegar, in awe of the way she'd calmly killed her father to save Landon's—and her mother's—life. She was *something*.

But she reminded him of too many things to name, and no matter what she'd done, she was still a little girl.

"Does your mom know you're here?"

She shook her head, casting a guilty glance at the ground. "But she doesn't understand. Mom thinks she's safe here, but she's wrong."

Henry's military training jumped to alert. *Danger.* He was good at stopping danger. But he also knew that poor woman who'd been tied up in a basement would be worried sick that her daughter was missing.

He pulled out his phone and texted Landon inside.

Call Sarabeth's mom. She stowed away in truck. Out here now.

"What are you doing?"

"Telling Landon to call your mom. He's got her number, doesn't he?" He hit Send on the text.

The little girl's face flickered for a moment. A wince, a moment of guilt, then sort of resetting herself. Focusing on him and this bizarre little stunt rather than all the trouble she'd no doubt be in.

"You have to protect my mom. She's in danger."

"How do you know that?"

She crossed her arms over her chest, a stubborn pout on her face. "I know."

He shook his head, trying to remind himself who he was, where he was and how little this was his problem. "Look, kid…"

"I may be young, but I killed my father. I don't feel much like a kid."

He understood where she was coming from. She didn't have a clue how much, but boy, was this little girl *not* his problem. "That doesn't make you Wonder Woman."

"See. This is why I need you."

"No, if you need anybody, and I'm not convinced you do, you want one of my brothers. Landon helped you before. He'll—"

"No, I need you."

"Kid—"

"You're mean."

Henry had his mouth open, but no words came out. Mean. He was indeed mean. Had been called it in a lot more colorful language than this little girl had employed.

"You're the mean one," she insisted. "Your brothers are nice, or at least nicer than you. Whoever wants to hurt my mom is mean. And real bad. She needs someone who can protect her from that. I'm mean, but I'm small. I need help."

Henry tried to harden his heart—after all, he wasn't sure he even had a heart anymore. Or if he'd ever had one to begin with.

But it hit close to a home he'd spent a lifetime running from. A failure he'd tried to make up for his entire military career.

And failed, more times than he liked to count. The failures always outweighing the successes, no matter how the scales tipped in his favor.

"Please," the little girl said, big eyes on him imploringly. "You're the only one who can help."

Chapter Two

Jessie Peterson knew she was driving too fast considering the last thing she wanted to do was get pulled over by the cops—God, she'd had enough cops this month to last a lifetime. But she had to see for herself Sarabeth was okay.

What had she been thinking, letting Sarabeth go into that store by herself? Never again. Never again.

You want her to have a normal childhood now, remember?

Well, that was stupid. Who got to have a normal childhood after they'd killed their father?

Guilt waved up and threatened to swallow her whole. She'd ruined Sarabeth's life. The past few months had been hell and she hadn't been able to save her only child. After ten years of keeping her safe—from Jessie's own father, from the man she'd thought would save her from all that who'd turned out to be just as big a monster— Jessie had failed.

Her breath was coming too quickly and she squeezed the steering wheel too tightly. She was letting guilt take over, and that was something she was working on in therapy.

But Jessie knew she'd failed her daughter. Because Sarabeth had run.

After some thought, it had all made sense. Sarabeth didn't like her therapist. Dr. Young had been the only choice for a child psychologist in the area, and Sarabeth had made it clear she didn't like him.

Jessie shouldn't have insisted. She should have worked with the social worker for another alternative. She should have done everything—

No, we're not going to spiral, Jessie. Because that doesn't help Sarabeth, does it? And your daughter needs help.

She would pick Sarabeth up from the Thompsons', thank them for watching after her and then she would have a long, calm talk with her daughter. Together, they would come to a conclusion that suited them both.

One that included keeping the Thompsons out of their lives.

Jessie knew she owed everyone at the Thompson Ranch. Landon Thompson and Hazeleigh Hart had both risked a lot to help Sarabeth. When they were under no obligation to do so. When they hadn't even known who she was. Sarabeth might have pulled the trigger that kept Rob from killing them all, but Jessie owed her life just as much to Landon and Hazeleigh as to her daughter.

It was Jessie's whole embarrassment at the situation that made her want to keep her distance. Her *and* Sarabeth's distance.

But Sarabeth was fascinated with the brothers, with the ranch and…

Well, if Jessie hadn't made her see Dr. Young today everything would be different. That was the problem, and that was a problem they could solve.

Jessie pulled to a stop next to a big silver truck in front of a beautiful old ranch house. The Thompsons' house—which had been the Harts' when she'd lived in Wilde—had been well tended, repaired and looked cozy and homey.

Or might have, if one of the imposing Thompson brothers wasn't standing on the porch like some kind of bad omen. Now she had to try to remember which one this was. Not Landon. Him she knew. The rest of them all kind of blended together.

More importantly, Sarabeth was nowhere to be seen.

Jessie got out of her car, trying to fix a smile on her face. "Hello, again."

He tipped his black cowboy hat. "She's in the stables with Landon."

Jessie let out a breath of relief. She didn't have to try to make small talk with the big, dangerous-looking cowboy. "I'll…go get her." But she might as well say the rest first while Sarabeth was out of earshot. She took a few unsure steps toward the brother on the porch stairs. "I am so sorry for her interrupting your day."

"No harm done." He flicked a gaze down at her. "Except maybe to you."

Jessie laughed, but it came out bitter. She didn't want to be bitter. She had to be a good mother, so Sarabeth could break this awful cycle Jessie had gotten herself sucked into.

"Yes, well… I was a little frantic. Landon's phone call was a relief. I'll just fetch her and leave you to it."

"You don't want to know why she was here?"

Jessie blinked. She looked at the man in the chest. He wore a black T-shirt that clung to, well, admittedly well-formed muscles.

She looked at the ground. She'd learned faking a kind of meekness kept anyone from looking too closely underneath. "I think I know, Mr. Thompson."

"Henry," he said. "Call me Henry."

She didn't plan on calling him anything. Because she was getting her daughter and leaving.

"You can look me in the eye," Henry said when she didn't say anything. When she kept staring at the ground.

Temper flared. It was a bad one, but she'd spent eleven years of motherhood learning how to deal with it. Hide it.

Funny how it seemed to show up inside her daughter anyway. And made Jessie proud, though it shouldn't. Still, Jessie wanted her daughter to be strong. To be a force of nature who'd always know how to stand on her own two feet.

But as for herself, she still had secrets to hide. She lifted her eyes to his, hoping none of the temper showed.

His gaze was a soft brown that seemed an odd contrast to the hardness around his mouth. The hardness of him.

"Sarabeth seems to think you're in danger. That you need help."

Jessie shook her head, panic darting through her, but she held a placid smile. Made it a little sad around the edges. "She's been through a lot."

"Yeah, that's what I figured." But he studied her face, and *that* was another reason she hadn't looked him in the eye. There was a watchfulness about the Thompson brothers she didn't like and didn't trust—no matter how they'd proven themselves.

"I'll go get her now." She started forward for the stables, just a few yards away. She could even see Sarabeth and Landon's forms next to a pretty black horse.

"If you need help, though…" He trailed off, but she kept walking. "Whole passel of us here have your back. And Sarabeth's."

Jessie stopped. They'd said that before. In the aftermath of Sarabeth's shooting Rob. The brothers, the nearly identical sisters, they'd offered help. But Jessie had thought they were just…being nice. Finding something to say in the middle of a bad moment.

But the bad moments were gone. She turned, too puzzled to pretend meekness and avoid his gaze. "Why on earth would you help us?"

He seemed to give it some thought, then shrugged. "Because help is what we do."

HENRY TRIED TO stop thinking about the Peterson women. The little girl meant nothing to him, her mother even less. Jessie had collected Sarabeth, and the girl had trudged guiltily to the car. She'd given Henry one last plaintive look as she'd crawled into the back seat of her mom's sedan.

He'd never answered Sarabeth's request. Landon had come out and Henry had let Landon handle it. Handle the girl.

Henry figured Sarabeth would get an earful from her mom on the ride home, and that would be that. Because clearly, Jessie didn't think she was in danger the way Sarabeth did.

Henry had to let it go.

But he couldn't get over the way Jessie had looked at the ground. Or the flare of temper in her eyes when she'd looked back up.

Not totally beaten down by life yet. Good for her. And God knew Sarabeth had enough life for twenty eleven-year-olds. They'd be fine.

No help needed.

When he walked into the kitchen the next morning, though, it was only Landon sitting at the table drinking his coffee in front of his computer. Henry figured he might as well mention it.

Maybe then he could stop thinking about Sarabeth's imploring expression and Jessie's spark of temper.

"Can we expect any visits from little girls today?" he asked, crossing to the coffeepot. Not quite enough to fill his mug. He scowled. Too many damn people in this house.

"Didn't know you cared," Landon drawled in response.

Henry merely grunted and took a seat across from Landon. He wouldn't push, because this concerned him not at all.

"After what you said Sarabeth told you, I looked into

Jessie a little last night. Just to make sure she wasn't in any major trouble," Landon said, without Henry having to push at all. "Just trying to get an idea of what kind of danger she might be in considering the evil husband is dead. And interestingly, Jessie Peterson never married Rob Currington—and there's no record of her anywhere after Sarabeth was born."

"Interesting or concerning?"

Landon shrugged. "Hard to say. Sarabeth didn't ask *me* for help, if you recall." Landon studied Henry with some suspicion. "Why *did* she ask *you*?"

Henry grinned the way that had people who didn't know him scurrying to do whatever he asked. "She said I was mean enough to handle it."

"Yeah, such a tough meanie, worrying about it the next day."

"Not worried."

"Sure." Landon grinned, and Henry knew better than to be riled up by that grin. It would just prove Landon's point, and Henry didn't plan on proving anyone's point.

"Don't you have your own house to steal all the coffee from?"

"Hazeleigh *does* make an excellent cup of coffee, among other things," Landon said with such self-satisfaction Henry couldn't hide his scowl.

Smug bastard.

"But I was turning it over with Hazeleigh last night, and she pointed out something. Hard to say if it's connected, if it means anything, but Rob Currington died thinking there was still some of this stupid bank robbery gold out there."

Before Rob Currington died. Before Sarabeth shot him.

"I can't help but think it's possible there's still someone out there after it," Landon continued. "You wouldn't think it'd be important, but Rob killed his own father over it. He might not be the only one."

"What does that have to do with Jessie and Sarabeth?"

Landon frowned. "I don't know, but anyone connected to it? I'd be careful if I were them. Maybe Sarabeth knows something about the gold, and that's why she thinks they're in danger. Hard to say. She didn't talk to *me*."

Henry scowled deeper. "I'm not getting involved."

Landon leaned back in his chair and studied Henry. "She asked for *your* help."

"You just said it's about mythical gold and old-ass bank robberies. Count me out. I'm interested in real problems."

"You have to go find out what Sarabeth might know, Henry. So we can all sleep at night."

"Got nothing to do with me," Henry insisted. "Some of us prefer to keep our nose clean out here hiding from the man. Besides, she saved *you*, Landon, not me."

Landon kept his gaze level, his expression bland. "If that's how you want to play it." He pushed away from the table and began to whistle as he washed out his mug and then sauntered out the door. "But I think we both know that's *not* how you want to play it," he called as he disappeared outside.

Henry scowled at the door, wishing he could prove Landon wrong.

Knowing he wouldn't.

SARABETH *HATED* BEING GROUNDED. She *hated* when Mom was mad at her. Most of all she hated when adults acted like they knew better when she was the only one talking any sense.

Sarabeth had been the one who'd been able to listen to her father's plans. Because he hadn't thought she was a threat. Mom had been hurt and tied up, but Sarabeth had been able to do whatever she wanted.

She knew things. But even she knew the things she'd overheard sounded, well, over-the-top. Adults would think she was exaggerating or making things up. Even Mom would be skeptical.

Sarabeth looked at the gold piece in her hand. She traced the rigid edges. It had been her good luck charm ever since she'd found it. Mom had survived. They were free of her father. What was better luck than that?

The problem was the rest of it Rob had been looking for. Sarabeth knew someone would come for it eventually, and likely her or Mom in the process.

The doorknob to her room turned and Sarabeth hurried to shove the coin under her pillow and sat up.

Mom stepped in. "I'm sorry," Sarabeth blurted. She wasn't really. Not about what she'd done, exactly. She was sorry about Mom being worried. Sarabeth figured it amounted to the same thing.

Mom came and sat next to her on the bed. She reached out and slid a hand over Sarabeth's hair. "I am too."

"You are?"

"I didn't listen when you said you didn't like Dr. Young because… Well, I don't really like talking to anyone about my problems. But it's supposed to be good for you."

Sarabeth didn't have a clue why they were talking about Dr. Evan, but if it got her out of having to talk to him, she'd go with it.

"Still, you should have someone you can trust to talk to. I'm quite certain family services will require it."

"I only trust you."

Mom's eyes got watery and Sarabeth didn't know why that was the wrong thing to say, but clearly it was. "Okay, I kind of trust Ms. Angie." Sarabeth looked carefully at her mother. "And the Thompsons."

Mom's mouth got tight and she sighed. "The Thompsons are very nice, but—"

"They've got the most amazing horses. I like talking to horses. Horses listen and they don't say dumb stuff about girls needing to be nicer than boys."

Mom stiffened and she got that look in her eye—the one that usually turned into yelling. Sarabeth always kind of liked it when Mom yelled.

"Did Dr. Young say that to you?"

Sarabeth nodded. "Yes. Yesterday. He wanted to talk about Dad when you left, and I didn't want to. But he kept asking and asking and asking, and I finally just said he was mean. And I said you're not. And he said that's because women aren't supposed to be mean."

"Well." Mom huffed. "We definitely won't be going back to him, will we? We'll have to talk to Ms. Angie about alternatives. But he is out. I'll put my foot down if I have to."

Sarabeth snuggled into Mom. She liked it when Mom

put her foot down about stuff. It started to feel like the old days, before her father had taken them. When their life had just been theirs.

But then things had gotten bad and now... Now things could be good again. As long as no one came after them. As long as they were protected.

Which meant she was going to have to try to find a way to talk to Henry Thompson again.

And beg him to help.

Chapter Three

Jessie had always loved horses, and she might have considered it luck, if she believed in such things, that she'd been able to secure a job that involved them. Driving the stagecoach around Bent County was like all her childhood dreams come true. Plus, she got to bring Sarabeth.

Who was currently pouting on her little perch on the roof of the coach because she hadn't been allowed to help hitch the team. Because she was still grounded.

Jessie climbed into the old-fashioned stagecoach and settled herself into the driver's seat, trying to ignore the wiggle of guilt. What Sarabeth had done was wrong, and she needed to learn that lesson.

Jessie clicked the horses into a slow walk. There were little stops around the route where she'd pick up people, but otherwise her job was to simply ride in and out of town. The advertisements on the stagecoach their own mobile billboard.

Wilde didn't look much different than it had when she'd been Sarabeth's age. This had always been the goal. Home—because Wilde had been stability. She'd lived with her grandmother for the first thirteen years of her life in the little apartment above the hardware store. When Grandma had died, there'd been nowhere to go. So her uncle had collected her and taken her to the Peterson compound in Idaho that had turned out to be hell on earth.

Such hell, she'd believed in Rob Currington's foolish promises and run off with him—thinking he'd save her. But he wanted the same thing her father did.

Gold.

It was still hard to believe the gold had been real, but she'd seen it herself. And now it was with the FBI or some museum and good riddance. The pursuit of it had turned all the men she came into contact with into maniacs.

She'd escaped that for almost eleven years. Running out on Rob in the middle of the night before she'd been stupid enough to say I do to him. But not before she'd gotten pregnant.

She sighed, sneaking a glance up at Sarabeth. She had Jessie's auburn hair and stubborn chin, but her father's hazel eyes and fair complexion. She had a sulky pout still on her face, but those eyes danced with anticipation. She loved her little seat on top of the coach, and she'd be grinning by the day's end.

Sarabeth was the single best thing that had ever happened to Jessie. Given her a strength and a purpose she didn't think she would have found without someone completely vulnerable who needed protection from the world.

But the girl was getting older, and less inclined to

be protected *or* vulnerable. Jessie thought of Sarabeth's stunt and scowled at the horses in front of her.

Less inclined to be protected by her mother, but certainly happy to ask a perfect stranger for help.

Jessie scowled even deeper thinking about Henry Thompson, and the way he'd said she could look him in the eye like he understood *anything*. The way he didn't seem to believe the adult in the situation—*her*—could take care of herself.

She'd been doing nothing but taking care of herself. And now the gold was gone. There was no danger anymore. No one needed her for anything. She could just… live.

Without big males and their quiet, condescending studies. Without cowboy hats and soft eyes on a hard face. She did not need protecting—because she was safe. And if it turned out she wasn't, she'd handle it.

As if stewing about him conjured him, Henry Thompson was there. Right there. Waiting at the next stop. Big and broad. She had had her fill of dangerous men and he was clearly in that same camp.

But her body was not getting her brain's messages. Luckily, her brain was irritated enough not to listen. She pulled the stagecoach to a stop and glared at him. "You don't really want a ride."

"Sure I do." He flashed a smile—one that seemed utterly devoid of warmth or charm. It was all surface and made her a little too interested in what he might be hiding underneath.

She supposed that was why it was effective.

"Enjoying the ride, kid?" he asked, shading his eyes as he looked up at Sarabeth.

Sarabeth scowled at him. "I'm grounded."

"Probably should be," Henry replied with a shrug. Then he moved like he was going to climb onto the stagecoach.

Oh, *no.* "You can't get on. You need a—"

He pulled the bright green paper out of his pocket. "A ticket? Here you go." He plopped himself next to her.

"This is the driver's seat. You're supposed to sit in there." She pointed to the actual coach. She caught her daughter studying Henry a little too intently.

Ugh.

"This'll do," he replied.

She wanted to argue with him. She was half tempted to push him out. But he seemed like the kind of man who lived to do the opposite of what he was told. So she'd have to swallow down the urge to bicker with him. She could play the boring, shy woman to be ignored when it suited.

She gave the reins a flick and pulled back into the street. Henry shifted, trying to spread out his long legs, but there just wasn't the space for his large frame.

Served him right.

"This is one weird town. You guys really make enough to cover the cost of the horses?"

"Yes, Bent County Stagecoach Company does just fine, thank you." She had no idea what the financials of the company were, but they'd hired her and paid her, so surely just fine. "What are you doing here?" she demanded, when he shifted again, taking up entirely too much of her space. And she didn't manage to keep the snap out of her tone.

His eyebrow winged up as if surprised by her temper. Oh, damn him anyway.

"Well, Sarabeth's little field trip yesterday got us a little curious."

"I told you, we're fine," Jessie managed between gritted teeth.

"Yeah, sure, and maybe you are. The thing is it's a little odd."

"What is?"

"You two don't seem to exist on paper."

HENRY WAS SOMEWHAT gratified to see Jessie's temper come up. Her eyes flashed. Her cheeks turned a pretty shade of pink. But it wasn't embarrassment. It was fury.

Good. Fury was good. She wasn't totally beaten down by life. He knew what that looked like.

"You looked into my *background*?" she asked on a hissed whisper.

"Technically, Landon did."

"None of you have any damn right."

Henry shrugged, unbothered. "Just making sure the kid was in an okay position."

"An okay position? An okay position?" He thought she was going to start yelling, but she disappointed him a bit. She sucked in a breath. Let it out. Her shoulders slumped and her eyes tipped down so he couldn't meet her gaze. She flicked the reins and expertly moved the horses along.

One more long breath and then she spoke. Calmly.

Quietly, with just a hint of apology in her tone. "Sarabeth is just fine. If you have concerns, you only have to discuss them with our social worker."

"Social workers," he muttered with disgust. "What can they do?"

"Plenty, if you let them."

He supposed that was the difference. A mother who might want help. His never had.

This wasn't about his mother. He looked up at the girl sitting cross-legged on a little perch on the roof of the rickety old stagecoach. She was studying him closely, and he—a man who'd faced down men with guns, entire terrorist organizations—wanted to fidget.

Her frank, childish gaze seemed a little too insightful.

Ridiculous.

"Look, if you don't exist on paper, you're hiding from something. If you're hiding from something, it usually means you're in danger. Why not let us help?"

She didn't say anything to that for a very long time. Her chin came up a little, but she didn't look at him. Her grip on the reins was too tight, but she kept her movements relaxed and easy.

She was a woman of strange dichotomies. Ones that didn't quite add up.

"The person we were hiding from is dead," she said after a few moments, in that same calm voice almost as if she was asking permission for it to be the truth.

He studied her profile, but she was careful of the angle, never giving him much of a view of her eyes. The color hadn't gone from her cheeks.

"But Mom…"

Henry looked up at the girl. She was chewing on her lip. Clearly torn between telling him whatever her mother was hiding and getting the help they obviously needed.

"There are no buts," Jessie said very calmly. "All this foolishness about this…old gold. I don't understand it. Even knowing it's real now, I still don't understand it. But the gold has been found. Rob is dead." She swallowed. "Sarabeth is dealing with the aftereffects of that." There was a hesitation, and then Jessie's voice lowered and she leaned close enough he could smell the flowery scent of her shampoo. "Her therapist says it's normal to still feel some danger, but I can assure you there is none."

Henry flicked another glance at Sarabeth. She was frowning, but he didn't think she'd heard what her mother had said or there'd be more outrage or hurt or arguments.

Jessie's shoulders were stiff, her eyes on the horses, and everything she said made sense. It seemed reasonable Sarabeth would have some paranoia. She had a social worker and a therapist on it, plus a mother who apparently cared.

He didn't need to stick his nose in their business.

But his instincts hummed that there was something missing. He should let it go. Really let all those military instincts go. He was a rancher now. Nothing more. Nothing else. Just Henry Thompson, cowboy.

He kept trying to convince himself of that as the horses clip-clopped along, the coach rattling behind them. It really was a bizarre town. Stagecoaches and old bank robbery gold, and some murders when there were barely enough people to murder and *be* murdered.

She pulled to a stop at the next little bench. She turned and smiled at him, eyes not quite meeting his. "Here's your stop."

He figured the ticket was probably for a round trip, but he didn't mind walking back to his truck if she wanted to get rid of him that badly.

He would be gotten rid of. He'd forget Sarabeth and her mother and *gold*.

But he glanced up at Sarabeth as he climbed down from the coach. She was frowning at him, and he remembered the calm way she'd recounted killing her father to the cops that night last month.

He was going to kill us all, so I shot. I didn't mean to kill him, but it's what had to happen.

Henry had envied her. A strange, twisted kind of envy, he knew. But it explained why he couldn't quite let this go, no matter how he should.

She'd done what needed to be done. Eleven years old, she'd ended the threat to her mother. And now she wanted his help, as if she hadn't solved all her problems.

Jessie cleared her throat and Henry looked at her. She nodded at where his hand was still clamped on the coach even though his feet were on the ground. "I hope you enjoyed your ride."

He said nothing, and he didn't let go. He wasn't sure… And that was the problem. This woman made him unsure when he'd never been unsure. She seemed to defy all his instincts.

"Sarabeth and I can handle ourselves, thank you."

Her smile was that same placid, timid thing, but something about those dark eyes didn't match. Almost like it was all...an act.

She flicked the reins and the horses moved, and he finally let go of the coach. It rattled away, and Henry frowned after them.

He had the very uncomfortable realization he might have read her wrong. That all his well-honed skills at first impressions and making snap decisions might have been completely off when it came to Jessie Peterson.

Worse, he had to agree with her daughter. They were in some kind of trouble.

It wasn't his problem. It wasn't his *responsibility*.

But that didn't seem to matter.

Chapter Four

The plan was simple. It would get her in a lot of trouble, it would hurt Mom's feelings, but it was simple.

Sarabeth studied her packed bag. She had everything she'd need. It would be a long, hard hike. It might even take days. But Sarabeth knew how to keep going, and she knew how to protect herself.

She was going to find the rest of that gold, *and* force Henry to help her mother. Because if Sarabeth went missing, Mom would ask Henry to come looking for her. She'd think about going to the police, but Sarabeth was pretty sure Mom wouldn't trust them no matter what. She might not trust Henry, or even Landon, but she'd ask them for help.

That was what Mom needed. And Sarabeth needed to find the rest of that gold. Rob had told her enough. She was pretty sure she could do it.

As for the Thompson brothers… She knew they'd find her. She had no doubts about that. She didn't mind being caught—as long as she got done what needed to be done before she did.

The hard part was getting out of the apartment with-

out Mom waking up. She was a light sleeper, but Sarabeth wasn't stupid. She'd planned and practiced.

The first step was the pillows. She threw them on the
floor, then eased off her bed and onto one. She pulled
her backpack onto her shoulders, fastened the headlamp
she'd gotten as part of a camping kit for Christmas last
year around her head. She didn't click it on yet. She
could get out of the apartment with her eyes closed—
and might need to when it was all said and done.

She stepped to the next pillow, then crouched down
and grabbed the first. She used the two pillows to soften
her footfalls to her closet—which she'd purposefully
left open. She pulled a sweatshirt off the pile, sat on
the pillow and got her hiking boots on, then she was
on her way.

She'd figured out the pillows softened the sound of
her feet—and kept the floorboards from creaking if
she stepped in the right place. Her biggest challenge
was going to be the doors. She'd spent time testing and
practicing how to hold and apply pressure at just the
right way to keep the doors from squeaking, but it was
still nerve-racking.

By the time she made it to the front door, sweat was
sliding down her back. Her heart was beating so loudly
in her ears she wouldn't have heard Mom behind her
at all.

But she kept moving forward. She had a plan. The
plan was going to help everyone.

She held her breath as she unlocked the front door
and snapped the dead bolt. She squeezed her eyes shut

when the click of the lock seemed to echo through the room and maybe the entire town.

But no lights flashed on. Her mother didn't appear. So she opened the door, and it didn't squeak. She was careful as she closed it, no matter how her hands shook.

She let out a long breath once it was shut. She wanted to run. To scream. But she knew she couldn't, and if she'd learned anything when her father had had her mother tied up, it was that she knew how to survive. How to handle scary things.

She had to be calm and careful. She couldn't rush and she couldn't panic. So she took each stair down with careful precision until she reached the door that would lead outside. She didn't have to worry so much about this one making noise since Mom was upstairs with a door closed, and the hardware store was empty for the night.

Still, she reminded herself to be careful. To be smart. And when she was finally outside, she allowed herself a moment to stand still. To settle herself.

She had a long way to go. This was only a first step, and there was no time to celebrate it. But she grinned to herself anyway.

Looking out at the town, all she saw was darkness, and though she could picture it in her mind's eye and knew where she needed to walk, things looked…weird in the dark. The shadows seemed to ripple with movement. They meshed together to form figures.

Sarabeth clenched her hands into fists. She bit her lip until it hurt so much her eyes stung. And then, she set off.

Sarabeth was brave. She was smart.

And she was going to make everything okay, once and for all.

HENRY WOKE UP to the odd sound of thudding. He rolled over in his bed, sure one of his brothers was doing something stupid. And hopefully not… He grimaced and sat up in bed.

The thumping kept going on, muffled enough it seemed to be coming from downstairs. Muttering to himself, he tossed the covers back and opened his door.

If anyone else sleeping upstairs heard it, they weren't interested in investigating. He thought of grabbing his gun, but if someone out to do harm was doing it this loudly, Henry doubted he'd need a weapon to take them down.

He walked down the stairs, wishing he'd grabbed a shirt. This drafty old house even made summer evenings cold.

It became clear as he got to the bottom of the stairs someone was knocking on the front door. He even heard the faint sounds of…shouting, maybe? A woman shouting?

At the same time he entered the living room, Dunne—whose bedroom was downstairs—was limping in. He was rumpled and looked as irritated as Henry felt.

"Who the hell is that?" he growled.

"Hell if I know."

Henry crossed to the door and opened it. Jessie Peterson stumbled inside as if she'd been leaning against it while pounding frantically. She righted herself and looked at Dunne, then at him. She seemed to decide he was her target.

"Where is she? Where *is* she?" She punctuated the demands by drilling a finger into his chest.

He grabbed her hand, because while her poke didn't hurt it didn't feel *great*, and he wanted to be annoyed and yell right back at her, but her hand was shaking. He kept it in his.

"Calm down, now. Where is who? Sarabeth?"

"Yes, of course, Sarabeth. She has to be here. She has to…"

Henry squeezed Jessie's hand hard enough to get her gaze to focus on him—no matter how angrily. "Take a breath," he instructed firmly, "and explain."

"She left. She ran away. She has to be here. She has to be…" She looked around wildly, her hand still caught in his.

"Dunne, why don't you go call the police and we'll—"

"No." She used her free hand to grab on to his hand holding hers. "No, you can't."

"Is your daughter missing?" he asked. Interrupted sleep and her sad brown eyes irritating him enough to have far too much snap in his tone.

She tried to pull her hand away, but he wouldn't let go. "You don't understand."

"So help me out here."

She licked her lips and looked around. Everything about her was panic and poor choices. They needed the police, but…something about her panic kept him from signaling to Dunne to do it anyway.

"I need you to find her, okay? Or Landon or who-ever. No one can know she's missing. You don't know what kind of danger she'd be in. Who might find her."

"Who might find her, Jessie?"

She sucked in a shuddering breath. And ignored the question. "She'd come here, I think. Maybe? Oh, I don't know. I don't know what she was thinking. She's never run away before."

"Before the other day you mean?"

"Yes, and she ran to *you*."

It was an accusation he didn't care for, since he hadn't done anything to encourage Sarabeth to come to *him* for help. Except maybe the whole stagecoach stunt.

"The police have the resources to—"

"So do you," Jessie said, cutting Dunne's calm words off. "I may have only been around town a short while, but I've heard at least six people tell me about how Brody found that little boy everyone thought was miss-ing. And helped someone with their missing father or something. You guys find things, help people and have convinced my daughter you'll help. She has to have tried to come here."

Henry agreed with her on Sarabeth's likely target being the Thompson Ranch, and as much as he be-lieved the correct course of action was to call the po-lice, he was also fairly convinced Jessie was hiding something—and *that* was why she didn't want to go to the police.

Figured. Not the protective mother she pretended. Just out to protect herself. He should have seen that coming.

Well, regardless, Sarabeth was likely in trouble. Trouble of the girl's own choosing, but that didn't mean he was about to leave an eleven-year-old to the wolves—metaphorical or literal. "Dunne, wake everyone up. Start a search from here. I'll take Jessie back to town and see if we can find a trail of some kind."

Dunne nodded, and Henry took Jessie's arm and led her outside. She went willingly, but of course not silently. "I don't know why we'd go all the way back to town. You and I both know she'd be coming here."

"Maybe," Henry agreed. "But what if she's not? We need the full story, and you were likely too panicked about whatever trouble you've gotten yourself into to worry about what Sarabeth was *actually* doing."

"Excuse me?"

He jerked his chin toward the truck. "Get in and wait. I'll only be a second." He hurried back into the house and up to his room where he grabbed a shirt, muttering under his breath the whole time. Jessie and her daughter were becoming trouble he didn't like.

When he returned to the truck, he was almost surprised to see her sitting patiently in it. He thought she might have bolted. Like her daughter.

She didn't argue with him when he got in, and she let him pull out onto the gravel road before she said anything.

"What do you think Sarabeth was actually doing?"

"Hard to say when you won't tell anyone the full truth."

She seemed to think that over. "There isn't much to the full truth. Some people who'd like to hurt me would hurt Sarabeth in my stead. I mostly think we're safe here, as long as we don't make any waves. Cops are waves. Besides, if the cops get involved, so does the social worker, and I think we all know what happens then."

"Seems to me if she was happy with you she wouldn't keep running away."

"Why are you acting like I'm the bad guy here?" Jessie demanded, and when he flicked a glance at her he was just a little puzzled to see actual confusion in her expression. Not defensiveness or outrage.

"You can't even call the cops when your daughter runs off because of some trouble *you're* in?" He shrugged. "Seems to me you should be more concerned about her over yourself, so sorry if I don't crown you mother of the year."

She heard the buzzing in her head, knew she should breathe with it. Look down, look away. It didn't matter what Henry Thompson thought of her mothering. Reacting wouldn't help Sarabeth any, and that was all that mattered.

Her little girl out there wandering around trying to get to the Thompsons for reasons Jessie still didn't understand. Not mother of the year? Oh, she knew exactly all the ways she'd failed as a mother. They looped through her mind every night when she went to bed.

But she also knew worse mothers. She knew abandonment and neglect, and she knew parental abuse at the hands of her father. So no, Henry didn't have any right to judge her on this.

She couldn't breathe, and she couldn't look away.

She could only say all the things she shouldn't. "You have *no* idea what I've done to protect my daughter. You have *no* idea what kind of danger she would be in if the wrong people find her. You think I care about me?" She laughed so bitterly it seared her throat. "You don't know a damn thing."

He was very quiet for a very long time. So quiet the only sound in the truck was her own ragged breathing as she attempted to rein her temper back in.

"Not half the shrinking violet you like to pretend to be," Henry said after a while.

She looked away from him, stared out the window at the inky dark. Somewhere out there her daughter was walking around. Alone. Somewhere out there, her daughter had run away because...

Why? *Why?* Didn't Sarabeth know if the social worker found out about this that she could be taken away? Didn't Sarabeth know...?

Jessie closed her eyes. She couldn't go through all the what-ifs. She just needed to find Sarabeth—through whatever means necessary. And if that ended up meaning the cops, so be it.

But not yet.

"She's very worried *you're* in danger, you know."

Jessie whipped her head to look at him. He had a contemplative look on his face, and he drummed his fingers on the steering wheel as he drove. His eyes were sharp and focused on the road ahead, but she could tell he was thinking everything through. "That's why she came out to the ranch the first time. She thought *you* were in danger."

"I'm not."

He turned those eyes on her. Something skittered in her chest, like fear but not. "It sounds like you are."

"You don't understand."

"You keep saying that, with no effort to tell me what it is I don't understand."

"Because it's none of your business."

"And yet you woke me up in the middle of the night to look for your daughter."

"Because *she* is fixated on *you*. And let me remind you I didn't encourage you to come hijack my stagecoach, look into *my* background. If you would have butted out—"

"What? Sarabeth would have just accepted that? Because she strikes me as a stubborn little thing."

Jessie hated that he was right, and she could hardly argue with him. He wasn't stupid, and no matter how much she wanted to blame him, what was going on with Sarabeth had nothing to do with Henry Thompson.

"She ran away. Clearly. So as much as I can think of a hundred terrible things that might have happened to her in the middle of the night in *Wilde,* Wyoming, I also know she's a smart girl who knows how to take care of herself." Jessie sucked in a breath. "She had a plan. A very well-thought-out plan."

"Then let's see if we can't figure out what it is? Maybe there's a clue in her room. Meanwhile, my brothers will start looking for her from the ranch moving outward. What time do you think she ran?"

Jessie looked at the clock. Three. She went to bed at eleven, sure Sarabeth was sound asleep in her bed.

"Three hours ago tops. She would have planned it, and I'm predictable enough. In bed at eleven, usually asleep by midnight."

"Not enough time to get to the ranch. Too much time to still be in town. She got a phone or anything like that?"

Jessie shook her head. "She doesn't have a phone, and I put all the electronics away at night. I checked to make sure she hadn't taken anything before I came out to find you."

Maybe he was right. Maybe it did make her a terrible mother for thinking it through enough to go to the Thompson brothers over going to the police. But all it took was a police report, an overheard radio message. Petersons after Sarabeth. Social workers taking her away.

Henry pulled up in front of the hardware store and Jessie immediately jumped out, her entire body buzzing with adrenaline and panic. "We live upstairs. She snuck out of her room, out of the apartment—my front door was unlocked—and then down the stairs and out this door. Which was also left unlocked."

"Show me."

So she did. She led Henry upstairs and tried not to get frustrated when he lingered or studied something as inconsequential as a smudge on the wall. Of course, the only reason she managed to hold her tongue was the fact he looked so…serious. Tense and ready to act.

It reminded her too much of those years in Idaho with her father.

She swallowed down that foolish skitter of fear and

opened the door to her apartment. She let Henry inside. His large frame was so incongruous in the small, feminine space.

Jessie pointed to the pillows on the floor. "She used these pillows to muffle her steps, I think. She'd been messing around with the doors lately. I thought it was just a game. I should have realized she was testing how to open and close them without making a sound."

Henry surveyed the room. "She really put some thought into it."

"If you're going to use that as another reason to tell me how horrible I am—"

"Honestly? The opposite. This her room?" He started forward, but Jessie stopped him. "No, that's mine. Hers is down the hall."

Henry studied her for a second, and she didn't know what that was about, but he nodded, then went down the hall and into Sarabeth's room. He immediately began to look at things, and then through things. He pulled her pink-and-purple plaid comforter off the bed.

"What are you doing?"

"Seeing if I can find a clue. A diary. A map. A list of some kind. Something that might clarify her plan."

"But her plan is probably just to get to you."

"When we returned her to you last time?"

Jessie felt the blood drain from her head. She had to reach out and steady herself with the wall. "What?"

"I'm sorry. I know it's not what you want to hear, but there's more to this than her coming to us. I think that's *part* of her plan, but it's hardly all of it." He pulled the pillowcase off her pillow, scrunched up the pillow then placed it on the comforter. He matter-of-factly searched her bed.

When he pulled out a little purple notebook, Jessie leaped forward and took it out of his hand. "No. No, we can't read that."

"Why the hell not? It might be an answer."

"But it's her personal, private thoughts. That she hid to remain personal and private. I don't go through my daughter's things."

"I respect that. When said daughter isn't running away in the middle of the night and we need to find her."

Jessie knew Henry was right, but she held the notebook to her chest. Tried to hold in those old, ugly feelings, but… "I know what it's like not to have any privacy. To have nothing that's your own. To feel violated and…" She was giving far too much away—of her past, of herself. But the idea of going through Sarabeth's things the way her things had always been gone through—to possibly make her daughter feel the way she'd felt like a prisoner, like she couldn't make a wrong move or she'd risk her *life*—it made Jessie sick to her stomach.

"She ran away, Jessie. Either you want to find her, or you want to protect her privacy. It can't be both."

Chapter Five

Henry didn't understand this woman, and that would be fine in just about any other scenario, but not this one. Not where he didn't know whether to suspect her of something or not. Not when he couldn't tell if she was fierce, protective mother or uncertain victim or even cowardly criminal using her daughter as a shield.

Henry always knew what he felt about people right off. He trusted his gut. He believed in his observations and conclusions without fail—and without question.

Until Jessie Peterson had come into his life. Who *was* she?

He'd thought she was protecting herself over her kid, not going to the cops. But she'd picked the smaller bedroom closer to the front door—and maybe it was coincidence, but Henry had enough tactical training to know if you wanted someone safe, you'd choose their bedroom farther from the door.

He'd thought this privacy crap was about protecting herself, but then she'd gone on about feeling *violated*, and he realized she likely just had some childhood hang-ups.

Join the club.

Bottom line, Jessie Peterson didn't make sense, and he didn't like it.

Jessie swallowed. She still clutched the sparkly little notebook to her chest. But slowly—too slowly for the current situation—she loosened her grasp and then held it back out to him. "I can't do it. I can't. But you can."

Henry took it. He certainly had no qualms about an eleven-year-old runaway's privacy. He flipped the diary page open.

And then he couldn't help but laugh, when it wasn't a laughing matter at all. In different colors, in different fonts, on every *single* page she'd written:

Like I would ever write down my plan.

"Why are you laughing?" Jessie demanded.

Henry held up the book, pages out, and flipped through.

Jessie sighed. "God, she'll be the death of me." But the word *death* seemed to sober her and certainly did him.

"But we do know there's a plan. She spent some time making and hiding this. She's a smart, resourceful girl. So we start from here. I do believe her end goal is the Thompson Ranch, but there's something else. There's something more. Isn't there anywhere else she'd try to go? Something else she'd want to do?" He continued to look through her things—because while the diary may have been a fake, that didn't mean she hadn't left some clues. No matter how smart or resourceful, she was still eleven.

"No. We haven't been here very long, but she says she

likes it. She still has this…need to protect me. There's no imminent threat, though, so I don't understand. I thought she knew I'd protect her no matter what."

"Maybe that's the point."

"What?"

Henry focused on rifling through her dresser rather than the growing feeling of…understanding or connection. The girl was nothing like him. She'd *killed* the man who'd threatened and hurt *her* mother. "She knows you'd protect her no matter the cause, so she's going to beat you to the punch."

"But there's no imminent threat," Jessie repeated.

Henry gazed up at her and gave her a pointed look. "You keep saying *imminent*, which means there *is* a threat. Or could be."

Jessie closed her eyes and blew out a breath. "I just want to find her," she said, and her voice wavered like she was *this* close to crying.

He really didn't want to deal with *that*. He wouldn't even have the first clue what to do. "We will," he said, with that old military certainty. Because he had no doubt he could find her, and he thought it unlikely she would have done something stupid enough to be irrevocable.

"She wouldn't have run away for the fun of it. Or to get away from me. I know that. I do." Jessie began to pace, and thank God kept those tears locked down. "There has to be a purpose. More than having you help me. Like you said, she'd have to know you'd just bring her back home."

There was nothing else in the room to give any clues.

The girl was definitely too clever for her own good. "Unless she's stubborn enough to think enough tries could change my mind."

Jessie studied him, far more obviously than she'd done before. Again showing off that side of her that was far stronger and more in control than she wanted people to see.

"I guess." She scrubbed her hands over her face. "I guess you're right. In which case we should go back to the ranch. Or try to follow whatever route she would have taken? We have to find her." But she watched as he sifted through the stack of books on Sarabeth's little desk—choose-your-own-adventure types, mostly about pioneer girls in the Wild West.

Jessie inhaled sharply.

"What is it?" he demanded when she offered nothing.

"When…" Jessie cleared her throat. "When Rob had me tied up, he let Sarabeth roam around. Obviously, she was worried about me, trying to get me free, but I think… I got the impression she liked it. Being on her own out in the wild. Like a pioneer girl, she said. And she does love those types of books." She pointed at the book in his hand.

He looked at it. There was a young girl in pioneer garb, all windswept, hands fisted at her hips, looking determined. "What types of books?"

"Oh, the historical girl out in the middle of nowhere on her own, making her own way. It's a whole genre."

Henry grunted and set the book down. He didn't know much about little girls' reading genres, so he'd have to trust Jessie knew what she was talking about.

"But that's not the point. I think she got into the whole…gold thing. She wanted to find it too. I know she wanted to me save more, but she liked those gold stories, and I think she believed Rob when he said there was more." Jessie chewed on her bottom lip and Henry found himself having to look away.

"Where?" he asked gruffly.

"That was the problem. He didn't know. And I don't know how Sarabeth would know."

"She wouldn't have to *know*. She'd just have to think she could figure it out."

"The Peterson house is still out there. That's where Rob was set up. Where he held me. I suppose she could think…there's a clue there. But it's falling apart. Dangerous."

"Yes. Falling apart. *Abandoned*. Which means she likely wouldn't be found, if she didn't want to be. Not too terribly far from our place," Henry mused.

"Maybe it's genetic," Jessie muttered. "And skipped this generation," she added, pointing to herself. But she shook her head vigorously. "Surely she's not out there chasing fake gold stories."

"It connects though. Doesn't it?" Henry asked. "The gold story and this not-imminent threat to you?"

JESSIE KNEW SHE was going to have to explain herself. She just didn't know how to find the right combination of words that would keep Henry from telling his brothers, the right way of framing it that would make it sound…a little less insane.

She'd tried before. When she'd run away from Rob.

When she'd been pregnant and scared, she'd tried to tell people what she'd escaped.

No one believed her. No one took her seriously. Because a bunch of men in Idaho dedicating their lives to searching for lost bank robbery gold from the 1800s in *Wyoming* and hurting anyone who might stand in their way *was* insane.

"Jessie."

"Yes, it connects. Sort of. But that isn't the important thing right now. The important thing is getting to Sarabeth before she hurts herself in that old place." She gestured to the door of the room.

She could see a slight hesitation and was worried she'd have to just leave him here, taking up too much space in her apartment, but he gave a firm nod and then strode out of the room.

She let out a long breath of relief and then followed him, out the front and down the stairs into the cool night. But he paused right in front of the building. He looked back up at it and then at her, the harsh angles of his face looking dangerous in the faint streetlight. "You should probably stay here. In case she comes back."

"No, absolutely not."

"Jessie, be reasonable."

He sounded so *aggrieved* her temper responded in kind. "Reasonable? My daughter is *missing*."

"Yes, and the reasonable thing is that someone stay here in case she comes back. Like we've established, she's a smart kid. Maybe she'll come to her senses."

"And like we *also* established, she's stubborn. I know

my daughter. She won't come back until she's done what she left to do."

"And what's that? Because it seems to me you don't exactly know what she's left to do, for someone who knows her so well."

"You keep throwing out accusations, but you don't know me. Why don't *you* stay here and wait for her to change her mind and come back? *I* will go find my daughter. It was a mistake to—"

The sound of a car door had them both looking over to the street. Hazeleigh Hart stood there, staring at them both. Jessie didn't know her well enough to interpret what that expression was, but Jessie didn't think she wanted to know.

"Hi," she offered, walking over to them.

Jessie tried to smile. Everyone involved had been nothing but kind to her, but old habits and mistrust died hard. It wasn't that she thought they would do anything to hurt her—on purpose—it was just that she couldn't let her guard down with anyone.

You already have with Henry.

Yes, because her temper had gotten the better of her. It had been a long time since someone had brought that out in her, and she didn't appreciate it. At all.

"Landon thought someone should wait here in case Sarabeth came back, but he figured Jessie wouldn't want to."

"Landon is right," Jessie said firmly.

"And he figured you wouldn't let Jessie go looking on her own," Hazeleigh continued, looking at Henry.

He nodded silently.

"So I'll stick around just in case. If that's all right with you, Jessie?"

All right was maybe a stretch, but it was better than no one. And while Jessie might not be able to trust anyone, she knew Sarabeth liked Hazeleigh. If she did come back—which Jessie estimated at a less than one percent chance—Sarabeth wouldn't run away from Hazeleigh. "Okay."

Hazeleigh smiled reassuringly and Jessie handed her the keys.

"Call Landon and tell him we think she might be headed for the Peterson place," Henry instructed Hazeleigh. "We don't want to miss her, so we want to fan out. Jessie and I will start here. A few start at the ranch, and a few go straight to the Peterson place."

"All right. I'll tell him. They've all got walkies, but you'll be too far out for that and for your phone for a while if you walk from here."

"We'll be all right."

"Good luck." She passed Jessie and gave her arm a reassuring pat. "She's a smart girl. Brave. She's going to be fine." Hazeleigh went past and into the building and Jessie felt like her heart was in a vise.

The more people assured her that Sarabeth was smart and brave, the more anxiety began to curl itself in her gut and solidify like a heavy weight.

She'd been smart and brave too. Careful and certain. And Rob had still found her, kidnapped her. Smart and brave was all good and well, but it didn't mean you couldn't make mistakes, or the big, bad world didn't have other plans.

"Come on," Henry said, waving her forward. "She'd want to stay within view of the streets until she could get somewhere where landmarks could guide her. So we'll take the straightest shot we can." He crossed Main Street and then walked through the alley between the post office and the bank.

They crossed the back parking lot, and then into the hardscrabble patch of undeveloped land. The moon shone bright above, the stars doing their graceful waltz around it. It was cool, but summer kept it from being *cold*.

"I did this once," she said before she thought better of it.

"Huh?"

It was an old memory, long forgotten in all the other things that had happened in that year. But doing it again, at night, reminded her. The open sky. The dark. That thrilling feeling of freedom and terror. "My grandmother... I lived with her where Sarabeth and I live now. My mother died when I was a baby, and my father left me with my grandmother. I knew I was a Peterson, and I knew people whispered about them, but I didn't understand... I wanted to see the house. I wanted to figure out... I don't know. What the whole *thing* was."

"Like mother, like daughter, huh?"

"I didn't care about the gold—I didn't even know about it. I was just searching for..." Even now as an adult it was hard to articulate. Some kind of connection. Some kind of root of who she was. She'd loved her grandmother more than anything, but she'd known she'd been a burden to the older woman.

"What is it with this gold?" Henry asked with almost enough disgust to match her own.

"I wish I knew. I wish I understood *any* of it."

He kept walking, farther away from town, deeper into the dark black of night. He seemed to have an inner certainty about where he was going, where his feet would fall.

She would have preferred a flashlight.

"My brothers have horses and four-wheelers. They'll likely get to her first. I've got a walkie on me, so once we get within range, we'll contact them for an update. No doubt she'll have been found. Safe and sound."

Jessie thought about that for a few moments. "So why are we doing this?"

Henry didn't say anything for a long while. She tried to match his stride, step where he stepped so she didn't trip over a bump or fall and twist an ankle on a hole or, God forbid, step on a rattlesnake and—

"Just in case," Henry said. And then she felt his hand on hers. "Come on. I'll lead the way."

He linked his fingers with hers and did just that.

SARABETH WAS TIRED. Her feet hurt, and the backpack suddenly felt like it weighed a hundred million pounds. She wanted to keep going, but her eyes were beginning to droop when she walked. If she took a wrong turn, lost sight of where she was and where she was going, it'd be pretty darn easy to get lost.

Real lost. The kind of lost where bears ate you and nobody ever found you.

She swallowed at her dry throat, her heartbeat picking up a bit at the thought of bears. She had bear spray though. She was prepared. She wasn't dumb.

But boy, was she tired and thirsty.

She shined her little flashlight on her watch. She'd been walking for three hours. She'd wanted to make it to four, but if she set her alarm and got started at sunrise, that would be better than getting lost now.

Sarabeth let the beam of light move around her to determine if this was a good enough place to camp. It was a little bumpy, but she had a tiny backpacking tent that she'd gotten for her birthday after *begging* Mom for it. They liked to camp and did it a lot, but Mom was a restless sleeper and was always moving around, waking Sarabeth up.

She'd wanted her own space. Her own pretend freedom.

And now she had it.

Sarabeth looked around at the dark world surrounding her, and though fear wanted to creep in, she only had to look up. The moon was bright and almost full. The stars winked like they were sending her messages of support. Mom said she had a great-grandma up there named Sarabeth who was always looking down on her.

So she didn't need to be afraid. She kneeled on the spot and unzipped her pack. First, she took a long drink. She couldn't help another good look into the dark around her.

She frowned, squinted into the deep night.

There was a flash of light far off in the distance. At first, she thought it might be lightning, but it was too small. Too…methodical. Just a little dot of light, on then off. Blink. Blink. Blink. Rest. Blink. Blink. Blink. Rest.

Was someone sending a message? To her? To someone else?

Sarabeth replaced her water bottle, got back to her feet and secured her pack.

One thing was for sure. She wasn't tired anymore.

Chapter Six

Henry would have moved faster on his own. He tried not to linger too much on that thought or let it frustrate him. It was what it was and after all, they were looking for *her* kid.

Not his problem.

And yet, somehow he was hiking through the Wyoming wilderness in the dark anyway. Holding Jessie's damn hand because God knew she didn't know how to hike through the dark like he did without breaking an ankle.

How *had* he gotten into this mess?

He used his free hand to pull out his walkie. Nothing but static still. They weren't close enough to get an update from his brothers. He switched walkie for cell. Still in the middle of a dead zone.

The only choice was to keep moving forward. Day would break soon. The horizon to the east was already beginning its otherworldly glow. The mountains shadows of darkness to the west—which was where they were headed. It was hard not to feel like it was a bad omen.

But Henry had weathered enough bad omens in his

life—it wasn't the omen that was the problem. It was how you dealt with it.

"There's another thing I don't understand about this whole thing." She was a little out of breath and he knew she was struggling to keep pace, but she wasn't about to admit it. He wondered if the attempt at conversation now was to help her keep her mind off sore feet or exhaustion.

"It's a long list."

"Yes. But maybe you can explain this one. Why did Sarabeth come to you specifically? I would have thought she would have gone to Landon."

He could read between the lines. Jessie would much rather be doing this with Landon. Probably thought he wouldn't push her to move so fast or whatever. Well, that was too damn bad, wasn't it? "She said I was the mean one."

"Oh, I'm sure she didn't mean—"

"You think that offends me?"

Jessie laughed a little. "I guess not, but it's hardly accurate. You're not nearly as mean as you think you are."

"You don't know me, Jessie."

"I know you're here. Helping me search for my daughter in the dark. I know you don't particularly like me, but you're doing it anyway, because... Well, I assume because you're good at heart, and because Sarabeth has certainly endeared herself to you and your family by saving Landon."

He had to fight the urge to drop her hand. To distance himself from her physically, as well as all the other stuff jangling around inside him.

"Doing the right thing doesn't make you good at heart."

She made a considering noise, but that was all. Henry had to bite his tongue from continuing to argue. Obviously, this was a stupid argument anyway.

So what if she thought he was a nice guy? She'd be disappointed soon enough.

Because there was a difference between the right thing—something he'd determined he'd always do a long time ago—and being a nice, decent Landon-type guy about it.

The mournful howl of a coyote interrupted the quiet buzz of nightfall, followed by a few yips. He expected Jessie to panic or react in some way, but she didn't so much as tighten her grip on his hand.

Then he remembered she'd said she'd done this herself as a kid. Made this trek. He supposed he could understand if you were running away from something bad—the kind of bad he'd grown up with—but he didn't quite understand it for young women like Jessie and Sarabeth who, it seemed like, had decent enough mothers or grandmothers raising them.

"Sarabeth has bear spray," Jessie said out of nowhere.

Henry supposed she was trying to make herself feel better. "That's a good thing to have." Considering he hadn't thought to bring any. Of course at night, they were more likely to run into coyotes or cougars. Now, that was one animal he didn't want to tangle with. "I figure as long as we don't run into a cougar we'll be just…" He trailed off and winced. Probably shouldn't have brought up cougars to the mother of a little girl wandering about the wilderness on her own.

"I know there are cougars out here, as does Sarabeth." She blew out an audible breath. "Of course *know* and *think about* are two different things." Her hand tightened around his.

He tried to think of something to get her mind off all the dangerous animals around them. "So you grew up here?"

"In Wilde, yes. Until I was thirteen anyway."

"Then what happened?"

"My grandmother died. I had to go live with my father."

"Not a prince, huh?"

Jessie laughed. Bitterly. "You could say that. I wish I'd made better choices so that Sarabeth would have had a better father than I did, but I was young and stupid."

"She's got you. Trust me. One out of two ain't so bad."

"Why, that almost sounds like a compliment."

"Doubtful."

She chuckled a little, but her following sigh was sad. "I wish I could agree with you. But when a girl has to kill her own father, what's worse?"

"Not doing it, and having your mother die because of it." He hadn't *planned* to say that. It was just a simple truth to him. But he felt the way her hand tensed in his, and realized he'd given away far, far, *far* more than he ever wanted to give away to anyone.

"Henry…"

He hated the way her voice sounded…soft. Like she

wanted to soothe him. Probably that decent enough mothering instinct she had going on.

That he wanted no part of.

"In the end, no matter how it messes her up, the other messes you up a lot more. And that is the story of why, I promise you, I *am* a mean asshole, Jessie. Don't forget it."

JESSIE DIDN'T HAVE anything to say to this odd turn of events. She hadn't expected looking for her daughter with Henry would give her some insight into who he was.

He'd laid it all out in very generic terms, but Jessie could read between the lines. She was an expert in weaving her own generic terms that didn't specify what had happened.

His mother had died, at the hand of his father in some way, and he blamed himself for not stepping in and doing something about it.

She supposed it made her soft, but that tragic backstory sure made it a lot harder to be irritated with the grumpy, abrasive man.

And it was sure a lot better than thinking about cougars and Sarabeth out here alone.

They kept walking, and the world around them got lighter and lighter. Until he was no longer the shadow she was clinging to, but the outline of a man with broad shoulders and confident gait.

God, she wished they could stop. She wished they'd find Sarabeth curled up taking a little nap so they could bundle her up and take her home. And once they did, Jessie was going to…

Oh, she didn't know. But she'd have to get through to Sarabeth somehow. Maybe she'd have to agree to look for the stupid gold. Whatever it took.

Whatever it took to keep her daughter from running off like this.

Henry took out his walkie thing and then his cell phone, one at a time so he could still keep her hand in his grip, grunting disgustedly with each.

"Still nothing," Henry muttered. He surveyed the world around them, bathed in the dim light of dawn. "You need a break."

She shook her head. "I'm not stopping until I've found her."

"You'll drop."

"Then I'll drop."

"And expect me to carry you around?"

"Until *you* drop. If that's what it takes."

"I don't drop," he replied, so certain. She would give him credit and thanks, when this was all over, because that certainty really was helping her keep it together.

"I guess we'll see, then," she replied as loftily as she could manage.

He studied her for a long while, with an intensity that unnerved her. It made her all too aware they were still holding hands, and his was big and callused and scarred. An uncomfortable little flutter centered itself in her stomach.

Oh, no. No flutters with him.

"You're not what you pretend to be, are you?" he asked, still scrutinizing her.

She didn't like that he could see through her, but he'd seen her at her worst too many times. Why wouldn't he? If he helped her find Sarabeth, she couldn't care *what* he saw in her. Sarabeth was all that mattered.

But Jessie was hardly letting him think he had the upper hand here. "Neither are you."

He dropped her hand. Finally. "Not pretending."

"Maybe you don't *think* you're pretending, but you are."

He shrugged as if he didn't care what she thought, but there was something about the way he'd dropped her hand, kind of suddenly. Something about the way he held himself now. He was always tense, but she was beginning to notice there were different *kinds* of tension in him.

This was the kind that wanted any and all attention off him.

"What's this now?" He strode forward, and she assumed he was trying to change the subject, the attention, but when she followed she saw what he was pointing to. It was a tiny little metal link—like the kind that was part of a key chain.

Jessie swallowed. Like the kind of key chains Sarabeth loved to keep on her backpack.

"Henry..." She didn't know what to say. What to do. She was frozen, staring at the little link as Henry picked it up.

He looked around, then began retracing their steps.

She didn't know how he knew where to go, but a few yards away he crouched. "Here."

Jessie came to stand behind him. There was the full key chain. A little plastic pig with a ridiculous grinning face right next to a big rock.

Henry picked it up, then stood and looked around. "She probably stood on this rock to get a better vantage point. Maybe slipped a little—she didn't hurt herself," he was quick to add. "Or she'd still be here or there'd be more indentations around the area. But the key chain probably hit the rock and broke off and she didn't notice."

"Why would she need a vantage point in the dark?"

Henry was quiet for a while, making the nerves already jangling inside her intensify.

"She might have seen a light."

"A light? Out here?" Jessie looked around. She couldn't imagine they were close enough to any of the surrounding ranches to see a light, but she supposed she didn't know that for *sure*.

He studied the ground, holding the key chain in his hand. "This way." He strode into a slightly grassy area, mostly laid flat by the wind that usually blew through this kind of valley. "She came this way."

"But this is a much harder walk. If she planned it out, she'd keep going the way we were."

"But something changed her course. See this?" He pointed to the grass. It just looked like wind-flattened grass to her.

"No."

"There's slight indentations here," he said, pointing

to a part of the grass. Then he moved a little bit ahead and pointed again. "And here. Footsteps. And not big enough to be adult ones."

Jessie still didn't see what he was pointing at, but she believed him anyhow. He wasn't going to lead her on a wild goose chase for the fun of it. So she followed him through the grass, watching him as he inspected and seemed to see things there she didn't.

"How do you know all of this?"

"I've tracked a few people in my day."

"Why? I thought you were a rancher."

He paused for a moment, such a short hesitation she almost could believe she was overthinking things.

"Did I say *people*? I meant cows."

He had *not* meant cows, but Jessie didn't feel like pressing him on it. She just wanted him to lead her to Sarabeth. So she followed him. Their pace slowed considerably as Henry was clearly being careful to look for his *indentations*. Eventually, they reached a place where the hardscrabble outcroppings overtook the grass.

"Where are we?" Jessie asked, hoping he hadn't lost her trail. Hoping desperately that this was right.

Henry looked around. "Thompson Ranch is due south. Peterson Ranch west. Town east. We've managed to go a couple miles." He checked his walkie again, but only got static. "It's okay. We've got some footprints here."

Again, he pointed. This time she *sort* of saw what he was pointing at. She never would have noticed those little indents—just in the shape of a crescent moon—

but it made sense they were the marks of the heel of Sarabeth's boot.

She swallowed as too many *what-ifs* tried to terrify her to the bone. "You're sure those are Sarabeth's?"

"Key chain, plus size of prints? Yeah, I'm pretty sure."

"Okay," Jessie said, letting her breath out slowly. She'd choose to believe him. To be relieved he knew how to track people—no matter how.

He climbed up the outcropping easily, then held out a hand to her. She frowned at it. "I am a Wyoming girl. I know how to crawl over some rocks," she said. She regretted refusing help almost immediately, because though she *could* climb on her own, her body was bone tired and wanted to give up.

But Henry standing at the top of the rocks motivated her enough to push through.

When she made it, he smiled, and there was that damn flutter again, but the smile softened up some of the hard lines of his face. Made those soft eyes twinkle with something other than his usual flat suspicion.

"She really does take after you," he said, surveying her next to him. "I think I've talked to her twenty whole minutes and she's always correcting me too."

"Well, it sounds like you need to be corrected too much."

His smile didn't die, but he looked out over the other side of the rocks. Wyoming stretched out before them. The rocks, some pasture land, and there in the distance...

Jessie knew that tree. The crooked fence posts, the sagging barbed wire. The scraggly grass. It was an abandoned family cemetery.

Her family.

"Stop," Jessie managed, grabbing Henry before he could start forward. Her throat was dry and it came out more like a croak as her heartbeat panicked against her ribs.

Henry shot her a questioning look.

"This is Peterson land past there."

"So?"

"So if she saw a light, and came here, someone is on the Peterson land. When it's supposed to be deserted. That is not good."

Henry swore.

Chapter Seven

Henry didn't like the jolt of fear that burst through him. "Look, it was just a theory," he offered, hoping Jessie would stop looking so pale and alarmed in the pearly dawn. "We don't know she saw a light." Though he was hard-pressed to come up with another theory for why she'd been standing on that rock.

And he was pretty sure she had been. He'd spent too long tracking people, hiding from people, searching for clues, to miss the story that these clues laid out.

But Jessie didn't need to know that. She might over-react or panic, and that would be the worst thing they could do right now.

Her hand was still clutched on his arm. "If she went toward it…"

"She's a smart girl," Henry said firmly, but his thoughts were right alongside Jessie's. Because Sara-beth *was* a smart girl, but also an impetuous and curi-ous one. She wasn't afraid of danger enough, because she'd gotten some confidence by doing what needed to be done.

A double-edged sword in an eleven-year-old.

"Henry, I know my daughter." She blew out an unsteady breath. "She'd go toward it. She's too... She needs answers and she gets them. But she'd be careful about it. She wouldn't just go charging in."

Henry thought so too, but he was glad Jessie's feelings—calm, no matter how she clutched his arm—aligned with his.

"So let's follow suit." He studied the area around them. This was the eastern edge of Peterson land. They should be getting within walkie range of *someone* soon enough. "We don't know where—if—she saw a light, but she wouldn't go right for it."

Henry walked again to the edge of the rocks and looked back the way they'd come. He studied the rock he thought she'd stood on, the angle of the impression of her fall. He couldn't pinpoint where she'd been looking exactly, but he could rule some directions out.

"The house would be straight through all that," Jessie said. When he returned to her side she was pointing out across the vast expanse before them. "That cemetery—"

"Cemetery?"

"Yes, what that barbed wire is around? It's the old Peterson cemetery."

Henry frowned and looked at the hardscrabble patch of land. There were little markers that he'd figured were just rocks. But they were arranged in a sort of pattern, he supposed. Cemetery made sense.

He suppressed a shudder. He felt Jessie's eyes on him.

"Surely you're not afraid of cemeteries?" she said, sounding faintly surprised.

"I'm not afraid of anything," Henry replied tersely.

"Do you think they're haunted? Are you worried about ghosts?" She seemed far too amused.

It poked at an old…not a *fear* exactly, but just all that pomp and circumstance and grief around cemeteries made for a bit of a discomfort, that was all. Even abandoned, sunken cemeteries that did indeed seem to be the perfect haven for ghosts or spirits.

Because he'd seen real hell and dealt with *real* problems. Ghosts were far more intangible than the reality of what he'd been through.

"I've carried dead bodies out of war zones, Jessie. I'm not worried about ghosts or phantoms or whatever the hell."

She blinked and he inwardly cursed.

"War zones," she echoed. "You were in the military."

He shrugged. Not exactly a secret these days. His brothers were always telling their women about what was supposed to be on the down low. Henry wasn't about to explain it to this woman who meant *nothing* to him.

"Well, that explains some things."

"Huh?"

"You just have that… I don't know. You just make more sense within a military context."

Within a military context. "I don't have the faintest idea what that means."

"Well, I'll figure out a better way of explaining it once we find my daughter." She pointed again. "I don't know the mileage, but I know past the cemetery is a straight shot to the house from that ridge over there. That was the path I took way back when."

Henry looked at the landmarks and tried to orient

it all into the map in his mind. He wasn't sure of the mileage either, but it could be a long ways. The Peterson spread was vast. But if Sarabeth had seen a light, it couldn't be clear on the other side of the property, so that was something.

"So if the light came from the area of the house, and if I was Sarabeth, stood there and saw a light and wanted to go toward it, but carefully, I wouldn't take a straight shot," Jessie continued. "But I wouldn't want to get lost."

"We're making a lot of assumptions here," Henry warned. But he was making the same ones in his head, so he couldn't argue with hers. "But if she followed the fence line east, it would take her more toward where that old schoolhouse was. Closer to our ranch. Would she know that?"

Jessie chewed on her lip. "I'm not sure. She spent some time at that old schoolhouse, so probably."

"Well, let's see if I can find some footprints or something." He studied the sharp cliff of the outcropping. It would require some fancy maneuvering. Somehow he could picture Sarabeth crawling down it with ease though. "You need help, Wyoming girl?"

Jessie sniffed. "No."

He tried to bite back a grin. Now *this* Jessie was a lot better than the one pretending to be someone who was too afraid to make eye contact. Not that it mattered what Jessie he dealt with. He was just helping her find her daughter. He didn't need to like her to do that or anything.

He made it to the ground, then looked at her progress.

She was being too careful, thinking too hard. What she really needed to do was—

She jumped. A surprisingly graceful and athletic movement. She landed easily, then brushed off her hands. When she looked over at him, it was a kind of snotty *told you so* look, and something low in his gut tightened.

Nope. No way. Not going down that road.

He looked away, down at the task before him. The task that had everything to do with Sarabeth and nothing to do with Jessie.

He started searching for footprints, evidence Sarabeth had taken this route. Had gone west like he hoped she had.

"Is this it?" Jessie asked a little farther out than he'd been looking. She pointed at the ground next to a patch of grass.

Henry studied it. Another little half-moon, not quite as clear as the ones above, but the ground down here was dryer, more susceptible to wind. "Could be." He studied the area around it, trying to find the next one.

But something…trickled down his spine. That old feeling he'd learned to trust—not just as a soldier, but as the son of a man prone to using his fists to make a point. So he stopped looking for footprints and studied the horizon instead. He saw the telltale flash of just enough movement to have his instincts kicking in.

He pulled Jessie to the ground, behind some rocks, and hell, sheltered her body with his. Who knew how well the rocks would act as protection. Might as well add him too.

"What are you doing?" she demanded.

The gunshot exploding through the air answered her question for him.

JESSIE WOULD HAVE screamed if Henry hadn't clamped his hand over her mouth. He had his entire body wrapped around her, pressed against the hard, pointy rock. It was an uncomfortable position. Pointy rock to her back, hard, large man to her front.

But someone had shot a gun. At them, if she had to guess. *Oh, God.*

"Don't start panicking, Jessie. Okay? We're not going to panic."

It was an order, and it kept her tethered to this moment. No panicking. No letting her brain tumble into the possibilities. They weren't shot, and Henry was here with his military background. They were all right. They would be all right.

She wouldn't think about all the Sarabeth what-ifs. She couldn't. She could only focus on… On…

"Take a deep breath," Henry said low in her ear. "Count to three. Then let it out. Same count. You hear me?" Somehow, cocooned inside the protection of him and the rocks, he gave her a little shake.

Another tether. She nodded and he took his hand off her mouth.

"Breathe. One, two, three."

She obeyed. She didn't know what else to do. The counting helped. Focusing on the numbers, something to do, rather than everything she felt. In. Out. She swallowed but her throat was dry.

"Why would anyone shoot at us?" she asked, her voice sounding far more shaken than she preferred.

"No idea. But we're going to find out. Don't move."

Again, she obeyed. He very carefully moved, keeping her pressed to the rock, but some of his body peeled away from hers as he tried to peer around the boulders.

But another shot exploded into the quiet morning, and he ducked back down as Jessie flinched and pressed herself even harder against the rock behind her.

He swore under his breath.

"Henry."

"It's far off. So far they can't get a good shot at us. Which is good. It gives me an idea of the kind of guns they've got, and where we'll be safe."

She wasn't so sure she believed him. If it was so far off why did he duck when the shot went off? Why were they hiding? Why was his body protecting hers?

But she didn't voice any questions. She much preferred his fake story.

He looked down at her. His eyes were dark, his expression grim, but he was clearly in charge. He knew what he was doing. She wasn't used to trusting people, but in this moment he knew how to get them through whatever this was. He'd been in war zones. He knew how to deal with people shooting at them.

And you grew up in the Peterson compound. You know how to handle danger too.

Yes, she wasn't some fainting, screaming dead weight. She could hold her own. Maybe fighting back wasn't her strong suit, but she knew how to avoid danger, didn't she?

"Do you have a gun?" Jessie asked, curling her hands into fists so she didn't feel tempted to grab on to him.

"No, but I have a knife. What about you?"

She shook her head. "Nothing."

He nodded, then reached down and pulled the knife out of his boot and handed it to her.

She didn't take it. "What about you?"

"I can fight with my fists as well as any knife."

Fight. Jessie had never been a fighter. She'd been a hider. A runner. Fighting? She didn't know *how*, and the few times she'd tried, she'd failed.

She couldn't fail Sarabeth.

"Look, we don't know where Sarabeth is. Maybe she's safe and sound at the Thompson Ranch," Henry offered. Another possibility that seemed just as unlikely as far-off guns that couldn't reach them.

"And maybe she's with whoever is shooting at us,"

"Maybe," Henry agreed, and his gaze held hers. "I can handle this. If you want to stay put. Or run. It's not a question for me. I can wade in there and make sure she's not there. You can stay right here, with the walkie or my phone. You can run. All of those are viable options for you."

For you. It shouldn't put her back up. They were clearly very different people. And he was right. "I'm much better at running and hiding than I am at fighting," Jessie said, but how could she do any of those things without Sarabeth beside her? "I can't run away from my daughter, Henry. Not with the possibility she's out there in the middle of this."

Henry studied her. "Sometimes running and hiding

are what a person has to do to fight." He took her hand, pressed the sheathed knife to her palm. "But sometimes, like it or not, you have to fight. You follow my lead, you listen to me, you'll fight just fine."

Her fingers curled around the knife. *Fight just fine.* She had her doubts, but Henry sounded so sure. Like he knew exactly what he was doing. She desperately wanted someone to know what they were doing when it came to finding Sarabeth and getting her home safe and sound.

Henry put his hand on her shoulder, gave it a squeeze. "I'm not letting anything happen to you or Sarabeth, okay?"

It hit her too hard, in the middle of *whatever* was going on. No one was ever looking out for them. No one ever cared if anything happened to them. Jessie had been on her own since her grandmother had died. It hadn't felt like an impossible weight until Sarabeth had been born, and even that impossible weight had come with a matching, overwhelming joy and love.

For a brief almost nonexistent second, it looked like panic crossed his face.

"Don't cry on me now," he muttered. "We've got a gunman to take out."

"I'm not going to cry," Jessie managed, though her voice was croaky and she had to dash a tear off her cheek. "I just don't understand why you're doing this."

He laughed, and the sound was bitter. "Yeah, me neither."

Chapter Eight

Henry couldn't concern himself with Jessie's...emotions or whatever. There was a gunman. Shooting at them, and though he hadn't lied when he'd said the shooter was too far away, without a far-range gun, to be a real threat to them, it was only a matter of time before they either advanced, or something escalated.

Henry would really prefer if Jessie stayed here, safe and sound, and he didn't want to analyze *that* at all. But if he could handle whoever was *shooting* at them, maybe Jessie could find Sarabeth. *Or* they could get close enough into walkie range to reach one of his brothers.

Were they close enough for the sound of the gunshot to carry? He didn't know.

And that was the problem here. He didn't *know*.

"What is going on?"

"I don't—"

"No," Henry interrupted. "You're not going to lie, or hedge because it could be a couple different things. We're getting shot at. There's a reason, and you know it. Now I need to know it. Quickly."

She frowned at him, that line digging into her forehead that he was starting to recognize as sheer stub-bornness. That they didn't have time for. But before he could tell her that, in not the nicest terms, she sighed. Her shoulders slumped.

"I don't know who's shooting at us, but they're on Peterson land. If it has to do with my family, this ranch, then it's this gold."

"You've got to be kidding me." Henry thought about just leaving her here. Walking right for the gunman and taking his chances. Because he was so tired of nonsense stories about old gold.

"You have no idea how much I wish I was," she said, and she was so serious. Hugging herself like she was cold even as the day warmed. "You have no idea how little I understand it. But my father has dedicated his life to finding that gold. Rob…became obsessed with it after working for my father. If I believed in curses, I'd say just the *idea* of this ridiculous *bounty* cursed people into insanity."

"Jessie."

"And look, I get it. You don't believe me. You think I'm being cryptic because…what? I'm a pain in the ass? I think I can handle it? No, it's because it's *insane*. And no one believes me. Then they wade in thinking that if there is a problem, that it's with some off-his-rocker harmless old man, but my father is a dangerous man. I escaped, and I keep a low profile mostly because he doesn't care about *me*, but if he thought Rob told me or Sarabeth something about that gold, then we'd become his prime target."

"This man is obsessed with gold we don't even know exists?"

"Yes. If anything, it only makes him more dangerous. It's all he cares about. All he's *ever* cared about, and if you live in that compound, it's all *you're* allowed to care about." She stared at him, then rolled her eyes. "I know you don't believe me. The cops wouldn't either, and worse, they'd put Sarabeth's name out there and draw his attention. Bad enough if family services let me keep her, worse if they didn't."

But it wasn't so much a matter of belief. It was more trying to untangle what was happening and line it up with her story.

He'd seen men obsessed with less. Who dedicated their whole life to something—*anything*—just to feel smart or important. Those things didn't have to make sense to anyone but the man feeling them.

"Explain this compound to me."

She looked confused for a second, then looked up at the sky. "I don't think we have time for that."

She wasn't wrong, which irritated him. They needed to deal with the gunman, find Sarabeth and then maybe untangle the whys.

"But know they'll do anything in their pursuit of this. They'll murder you. They'll murder me. They'll…"

She trailed off, but he knew what she'd been trying to say. Sarabeth, too.

He couldn't get his mind around the whole *find gold* thing, but he understood people who wanted to kill. *That* he had far too much experience with.

And they were just indiscriminately shooting at people. They couldn't possibly know what he and Jessie were up to…

Unless they had Sarabeth.

"There's no other reason they could be out here? Shooting at us?"

"None that I know of."

He wished that made him feel better. But gold or some secret reason, someone was shooting at them while Sarabeth was somewhere out here. Henry had to find her—first and foremost.

"Okay, this is what we're going to do. You're going to stay here. I'm going to go find Sarabeth. She can't be far. If she was smart, she'd be hiding at daybreak. We should have caught up to her, generally speaking."

"But—"

"No buts. She's the goal, right? We don't care about gold or your father or whoever is shooting at us. We care that Sarabeth and you are safe. So you'll stay put." He pointed at the knife. "Someone comes, you use that on them, fight like hell, do what you have to. If they end up taking you back to that house, know I'll come get you out."

She looked up at him, eyes wide, but he didn't see what he'd hoped. Agreement. Trust. There was a wariness in there. And something worse than fear. Resignation.

"All that matters is Sarabeth is safe."

"Once she's safe, I'll come get you out. *If* it comes to that." And he had a bad feeling he'd do everything in his power to make sure it didn't.

SARABETH HEARD THE gunshots and froze. She knew what those sounded like now. What they felt like. She knew how to use a gun. She knew how to kill someone.

And still, everything inside her went cold and stiff. Why was someone shooting? *Who* were they shooting at?

She huddled deeper into the little shelter she'd made around a big boulder, an old tree and some fence posts.

Last night she'd kept that blinking light in her line of sight but hadn't gotten anywhere near it. She wanted to know who was out there—on Peterson land—but she'd known better than to get close. She thought whoever had the light was at the house, so she planned on going there once it was dark again.

But as soon as the sun had begun to rise, she'd known the best thing for her to do was hide. And so she'd been sitting here waiting. Planning. Dozing.

If someone was at the old Peterson place, they had to be looking for the gold. *Had* to be.

But who were they shooting at? Now that it was daylight and she was hidden away, the gunshots were too far away to be about *her*.

Mom.

No, Mom wouldn't be… Sarabeth chewed on the collar of her shirt. Mom would come after her, but she'd ask for help. Henry or Landon or someone. And they knew how to handle men with guns.

Unless Mom *hadn't* asked for help.

Sarabeth squeezed her eyes shut. Everything had gotten all messed up. There weren't supposed to be people here. What should she do now? At night she could handle herself. She was small and careful and could hide. She knew the house now too, since Rob had let her run loose in there when he'd had Mom tied up.

But she didn't know what to do about men shooting in broad daylight, knowing Mom was probably looking for her by now.

Mom had to have asked the Thompson brothers for help. *Had* to have.

But if she hadn't… Well, maybe Sarabeth needed to get to them. When she'd been watching the light last night, she had taken a route that would keep the light in sight while leading her in the direction of the fence line between Thompson and Peterson land. Surely there wouldn't be anyone between her and the Thompsons.

She could make a run for it. Just go as fast as she could and get the first Thompson brother she saw. They could help. They could get Mom out of any trouble.

Unless she's been shot.

Sarabeth wanted to cry at the thought. She nearly jumped to her feet and just started to run. Who cared what happened to her? She just wanted to get to her mom and make sure she was okay.

But she took a deep, gulping breath, because Mom always told her to breathe before she did anything stupid. *A smart woman thinks before she acts.*

Sarabeth had to think. She was smart. She was brave. She took another breath and squeezed her eyes shut so she could think about what to do rather than those two echoing gunshots that had interrupted her nap.

She gathered her things, carefully and quietly. She

shrugged into her backpack and thought about where she was and where she wanted to go.

The shooting probably came from the house. She'd have to go closer to the house. Make sure Mom wasn't there. Make sure that was where the people and the lights were.

But…what if she could get the people with the lights *away* from the house? *Away* from Mom, if Mom was out there? She chewed on her bottom lip and then decided that nothing mattered except helping Mom.

She dug in her backpack, came up with the matches, then set about building a fire. She'd make it small, but lots of kindling. She'd do what she could to get it going enough to start a fire signal. Someone would see the smoke and come help.

She used anything she could find—grass, branches, leaves, what splinters of wood she could pull off the old fence posts. She was old hat at building a campfire, but making sure the smoke built and rose was a little trickier than she was expecting.

She was sweating by the time she was satisfied. Still not certain it was big enough, but it had to be. Had to be. She stepped back to survey the smoke and the fire one last time.

"Keep going," she muttered. She fingered the gold coin in her pocket. "Bring me luck," she whispered.

Then she turned, ready to run for the house. She was far enough away from it and where she thought the shots were coming from that she could run for a little bit without anyone hearing her. Then she'd slow down, take it easy.

If Mom was hurt, she'd get to her. And find a way to help her. Save her. She would do whatever it took.

One more deep breath, and then she took her first step. But something stopped her.

No, not something.

Someone.

Someone had grabbed her backpack, stopping her forward progress. Keeping her still and then nearly lifting her up off her feet.

"Where do you think you're going?"

JESSIE KNEW WHAT it was to wait. In silence. In fear. She had learned in those teenage years to find a center of calm, no matter what threats were leveled against her.

But she could never find that calm when it came to what threats were leveled against her daughter.

Henry had ordered her to stay put. She had the knife he'd given her unsheathed in her hand. She was supposed to fight like hell if anyone came over the ridge of rocks.

If only she knew how.

But if it was for Sarabeth, she would. Whatever it took. And Henry would find Sarabeth. He'd promised, and he'd looked so competent wading out into the open world around them. Like he wasn't afraid of gunshots or imbalanced men with unhealthy obsessions they were willing to kill over.

She didn't really believe promises anymore, but she did believe in Henry's ability. She just kept hearing him say he'd carried men out of war zones. She knew he'd suffered through his father's killing his mother and felt guilty over it.

She knew he understood—in a way so many people couldn't—what the danger really was. Maybe he didn't believe her about the gold. She didn't need him to.

Because he knew what to do with a gunman, and understood Sarabeth was the goal.

It was just hard, because Jessie had never in her life thought to sit tight and wait for someone else to handle something for her. Her entire adolescence at her father's compound had been about hiding, then planning how to get out.

There'd been that brief, stupid moment where she'd thought Rob was the answer, but after she'd escaped *him*, her life had been about keeping Sarabeth away from her family. The gold obsession. The off chance her father might want something from her someday.

Maybe thinking she could make a home in Wilde had been a stupid moment too. She'd just assumed if he didn't *live* in Wilde, didn't spend time looking in Wilde, he didn't really care about it. And whatever gold was still missing—if he believed that—surely was somewhere else.

Anywhere else.

She frowned as she thought over Henry's reaction. Usually people rolled their eyes, scoffed, made fun. Or worse, they agreed with her in that way that suggested they might call a psychiatrist and have her involuntarily committed.

But Henry hadn't done any of those things. He'd considered. She wasn't sure she'd convinced him, but he'd *listened*. And while he'd asked if there was some other reason this could all be going on, he hadn't dismissed her out of hand.

Jessie had to resist the urge to peek out of her little makeshift cover. She wanted to see if those gunmen had come for her. If she could still catch sight of Henry out there. She wanted to...

She heard...something. Something new. The faintest exhale. Maybe a footstep? A rustle. She clutched the knife, positioned her back to the rock and her face to the opening.

She would fight. She could fight.

But when the person appeared, she could only stare. Her fingers went so nerveless she nearly dropped the knife. Catching herself at the last moment. But still, she couldn't fight. She couldn't even speak.

Because the woman standing in front of her looked... *exactly*...like Jessie herself.

Except she had a gun in her hand instead of a knife.

Chapter Nine

Henry held Sarabeth by the straps of her backpack. Once he was sure she wouldn't run or scream, he set her down on her feet.

She must have recognized his voice because she immediately turned and threw herself at him. Her little arms wrapping around him so tightly he could only stand stock-still. Then she began to cry.

Hell.

"Aren't you supposed to be too old for this?" he asked, looking down at her. Her hair had fallen mostly out of its bands and was a bird's nest of reddish tangles. Her hands were clutched in the sides of his coat.

Apparently that was the wrong thing to say because she only cried harder.

"Okay, okay," he muttered. He awkwardly patted the top of her head and looked around helplessly. He'd never been around kids. Granted, he'd been to war and seen grown men cry, but he didn't know what to say or do around a little *girl* crying.

"Mom asked you for help," she said between little hiccupy breaths.

"Well, yeah." The head wasn't working so he tried patting her back instead and peeling one of her hands off his coat.

"She's safe, right?" She looked up at him, her dirt- and dust-covered face streaked with tears. One hand was still clutched in his coat. Her hazel eyes were wet and imploring and something…something seemed to turn over in his chest.

"Yeah, kid." He rested his hand on her shoulder and it didn't feel quite so awkward when she leaned into him. "Let's get back to her, huh?"

She nodded. "But I heard guns."

"Yeah, so did we, but we haven't quite figured out where or why." It was a little bit of a lie, but not a total one. "Come on."

She finally let go of his coat, and he expected her to follow him, but instead, she curled her hand around his. Like it was natural. Normal. Henry didn't have the slightest idea what to do with it.

In the end, all he could do was curl his own fingers around hers and try not to think about how small and vulnerable her hand seemed in his much bigger one. He eyed the horizon and made sure to position himself between Sarabeth and whatever direction the house was. It wasn't foolproof safety, as the gunmen could have moved from the house, but he tried to walk where there was cover.

And he kept on full alert, ready to keep her safe from any gunshots as they walked back to where Jessie was hiding.

"You're really bad at dealing with people crying," she said, using her free arm to wipe her nose.

Henry frowned down at her. He *knew* that, but somehow her saying it rankled. "Yeah, well, people don't usually cry around me. What was I supposed to do?"

"You're supposed to say it's okay. Be encouraging. And the back pat wasn't bad, but a rub is better."

"Well, I'll keep that in mind next time you start the waterworks all over me." God, he hoped this was the one and only time.

"I don't cry very often, but I was worried Mom came and looked for me by herself when I heard those gunshots. That she might be hurt."

"And whose fault would that have been?" He winced. That was a dumb thing to say to a kid.

But she shrugged. "Exactly. But she got you. So everything's going to be okay."

The idea that everything was going to be okay simply because he was here did not sit well with him. At all. He had a lot of confidence in his abilities, but there were a lot of variables here—including this little girl he didn't know what to do with.

He studied his surroundings again. He needed to get Jessie and Sarabeth back to the ranch. Then he and one of his brothers could get to the bottom of the shooting. Maybe even bring in the cops if he got Jessie and Sarabeth out of it. Leave out crazy gold stories and just bring up the gunshots.

It was a plan anyway. And if he focused on that he didn't have to think about the little girl's hand in his.

Like she was sure he was going to swoop in and make everything okay for her and her mom.

Like she knew, deep down under all the reasons he told himself this didn't matter to him or have anything to do with him, that was exactly what he wanted.

They didn't walk back the way Henry had come. He took a more careful route, did his best to hide their tracks so no one could track *them* the way he'd tracked Sarabeth.

They hadn't been too off the mark, he and Jessie. Sarabeth hadn't been more than a half mile away, and toward the Thompson Ranch. He looked down at their joined hands, and wanted to keep his mouth shut but...

"You did good, kid. Good job hiding. Good job staying away from the light."

"You saw it too?" she asked, angling her face up toward him. "The blinking light?"

"Blinking?"

"Yeah, three blinks then a break then three blinks. It kept going. Three. Stop. Three."

Henry frowned over that. Blinking lights pointed more to a signal than simply just light to see by. But Sarabeth kept talking.

"I wanted to know what it was, but I figured it'd be better to wait for daytime when I could see. So I just kept it in sight and kept walking. I wanted to be close enough to you guys's place that I could run there. But when the sun came out I figured I'd better hide." She paused, studying him carefully as they walked. "I really did a good job?"

"I mean, running away was stupid. But after that colossal mistake, you made some good choices."

She grinned up at him. Which had that thing turn over in his chest again. Something was seriously wrong with him.

"What were you up to, Sarabeth?"

She chewed on her bottom lip. "Wellll…"

"Might as well spill it now that you've gotten yourself in a heap of trouble."

She sighed, her shoulders slumping. Then she dug her free hand into her pocket and pulled something out. She held it to him so he took it.

A coin. An old…gold coin. Henry swore. "You've got to be kidding me."

"There's more of it. My father was sure of it. And I know Mom's family wants it, and I just thought if I could find it, we wouldn't really be in danger anymore. And it would be ours. Not theirs."

Henry turned the coin over. It was real gold, that was for sure, but he didn't see why all these people were willing to kill over it.

"Can I have it back?" She held out her hand. "It's my good luck charm."

He handed it back to her as they walked. "There ain't no such thing as luck, Sarabeth."

She scrunched up her nose. "I think you're wrong."

Henry shrugged. No point arguing with an eleven-year-old. But she should know… "Look, maybe there's luck. Maybe there's not. But you can't rely on it either way. End of the day, you can only rely on yourself."

She studied the coin, then him. "I can rely on my mom."

It gave him a little pang. What must *that* be like? But he was a grown man. No need to be thinking about old mommy issues when there was a shooter out there, and he needed to get Sarabeth and her mother safe.

They started to approach the place where he'd left Jessie, but Henry slowed. Something was wrong. The sound of…movement. More than the wind. More than an animal.

"Get behind me," he ordered in a quiet whisper.

"But—"

He moved Sarabeth behind him and held her there, and was glad when she had the presence of mind to not say any more. He stayed very still, trying to get a handle on what was wrong.

A voice. Female, so he supposed it could be Jessie talking to herself, but that seemed wrong too. "Stay put," he muttered, arranging Sarabeth so she was seated behind a boulder. "Don't move or make a sound."

She looked at him with a rebellious frown but nodded once. He'd have to take her word for it.

He didn't see anything. Didn't *feel* anything. Though he sort of suddenly hoped good luck existed and lived within Sarabeth's little coin because none of this made sense.

Another shuffle, the low murmur of voices. Henry crept forward, from the back of the rocks. If he climbed up, he could look down and see what was what. But he had to be careful, and silent.

Luckily he had experience with just that, and though

it took longer than he might have wanted he made it to the top without disturbing so much as a pebble. He peered into the little place he'd left Jessie. She was there, and there was some relief that she appeared whole and unharmed.

But she wasn't alone.

He looked back at Sarabeth, who was crouching like he'd told her to, with wide eyes and a worried frown on her face. But she'd listened.

He retraced his steps. Once he was close enough to whisper, he posed his question. "Does your mom have a...twin sister?"

"No," Sarabeth replied.

"Someone who looks just like her?"

Sarabeth shook her head.

Henry looked back at where he'd just been. This didn't make sense. There were two identical women. Henry wasn't even sure he'd have been able to tell them apart.

If one wasn't holding a gun.

EVEN THOUGH A gun was pointed at her, all Jessie could do was stare at the woman's face. Searching for some kind of difference. A scar, a mole, a wrinkle.

It was impossible. Granted, she didn't spend a lot of time *looking* at her own face, but still. It was so darn bizarre she was having trouble paying attention to what the woman was saying.

"Who *are* you?" Jessie finally asked. What else was there to do? She supposed try to get the gun, or fight with the knife still in her hand, but...but... "Why do we look exactly alike?"

The woman didn't seem surprised to find a carbon copy of her hiding out on Peterson land. But there must have been some suspicion and maybe a little confusion in her mind, because she certainly didn't start shooting or ordering Jessie to do anything.

She glanced up at the rocks surrounding them, her suspicious frown smoothing out carefully before she returned her gaze to Jessie. "Are you out here alone?"

Jessie hesitated, which was a mistake. She knew it just by the way the woman looked at her. It reminded her far too much of her father. "More or less."

The woman snorted. "Uh-huh." She seemed to consider, then she stepped to the side. "Come out here."

Jessie swallowed and tightened her grip on the knife. Out there seemed safer—after all, she could run out there. Here she was trapped by rocks and the woman with the gun.

But still. Following orders could be dangerous.

"Now," the woman said, holding the gun just a little tighter.

"I think you should tell me what's going on." But Jessie moved a little forward, and she didn't drop the knife.

Again, the woman snorted. "I'm guessing I don't know much more than you."

"I find that *very* hard to believe."

The woman shrugged, then motioned with the gun. "Come on. Someone's out here. Probably trying to break you out of my evil clutches. If it ain't one of mine, it's one of yours."

"I don't—"

The woman whirled, but she was a second too late.

Henry had the gun out of her grasp so quickly Jessie wasn't even sure how it had happened. And then she didn't care, because Sarabeth darted forward and flung her arms around Jessie's waist.

Jessie hugged her back fiercely. For a few precious moments nothing else mattered except her daughter was safe and in her arms. "You're okay?" She pulled her back enough to study her.

Sarabeth nodded. Her eyes were uncharacteristically red-rimmed and Jessie's heart tightened. Sarabeth didn't cry easily. She pulled her back into a tight hug.

"You are in so much trouble," Jessie managed through her tight throat. "So much."

Sarabeth squeezed tighter. "I'm sorry, Mom."

Jessie pulled back again, needing to study Sarabeth's face in more detail. Catalog every freckle, every scratch. "No more doing it on our own, okay? We're in this together. No matter what. Promise?"

Sarabeth's hazel eyes were wide, but she seemed to give it some serious thought. She took a deep breath. "Okay, I promise. If you do."

Jessie hesitated. She was the mother. Didn't that mean sometimes she had to act alone—to protect? Didn't that mean that they weren't always a team of equal partners, even if she wanted Sarabeth to feel like they were?

But that wasn't fair. Jessie wasn't sure how to be *fair* as a mother, though. "We are *always* a team. But sometimes I'm the leader of the team, and make decisions for the both of us, okay?"

Sarabeth wrinkled her nose, but before she could

agree or argue, Henry cleared his throat, and everything else came crashing down.

Right. This wasn't over. Jessie stood.

Henry was holding the identical woman's hands behind her back. She looked…bored, rather than scared or irritated. And she looked a little too hard at Sarabeth.

Jessie stood between them. "Why don't you tell us who you are?"

The woman seemed to give this some thought. In fact, everything about the woman wasn't so much bored as…calculating. "Quinn."

"Quinn Peterson?"

"How very observant."

Jessie frowned. "What are you doing here? Why do you look like me?"

"And what are you after?" Henry added.

"That's a *lot* of questions, guys."

"Were you the one shooting?" Sarabeth asked, her head peeking around Jessie's body.

"Now, that is a good question," Henry said. "Answer that one first."

"Today? No, I wasn't the one shooting."

"Then who was?" Henry demanded.

"How about this? You get me out of here without any more people shooting at us—or at least without me getting *shot*—I'll tell you everything you want to know."

Henry's gaze flicked to Jessie's. He was leaving it up to her.

"Why do you need to get out of here?" Jessie asked.

The woman rolled her eyes. "God, the questions with

you people. Isn't it obvious? Shooting? Bad guys hiding in falling-down houses. Et cetera."

It didn't add up, Jessie knew. Why would this woman need help getting out of here if she was wandering around on her own with a gun? A gun she was more than willing to point at Jessie before Henry had gotten ahold of it.

But she likely had answers. And clearly Henry could handle the woman. She gave Henry a little nod.

"All right. You two, get behind me. Our friend here will lead the way."

Sarabeth scurried to do as Henry instructed, but Jessie...hesitated. This all felt like Peterson and gold nonsense and it felt wrong to get Henry wrapped up in that. He might not believe it, but anything that connected to her father was dangerous. Maybe Henry could handle it, but it didn't—

"Jessie." She looked up at him. His dark eyes were serious, but not...angry. And when he spoke, she couldn't puzzle out his tone, but it wasn't demanding or commanding. "Go on now." There was a softness to it, and to him, in the way he nodded at Sarabeth.

Or she was losing her mind from exhaustion. But still, she didn't know what else to do but move behind Henry.

He let go of the woman's—*Quinn's*—hands. He patted her down like she'd seen police officers do on television shows.

"At least buy me a drink first," Quinn quipped.

Henry ignored her, finished the pat down, then stepped back toward Jessie and Sarabeth. He pointed the gun at her. With Jessie and Sarabeth behind him, he gestured at the horizon. "You'll walk in front of us. Straight ahead till I tell you otherwise. Make a wrong move, I can't promise I won't be the one shooting at you."

She grinned at Henry. Flirtatiously. "Don't make promises you can't keep, big guy."

Something…acidic curled in Jessie's chest, so odd and foreign she didn't know what it was. So she simply took Sarabeth's hand in hers.

"Go on now. Straight ahead," Henry said.

Quinn shrugged and began to walk. So Henry began to follow, and then Jessie and Sarabeth. When he wanted Quinn to move in a different direction, he told her right or left or to walk toward a tree. Jessie watched him more than the woman. He was alert, watching every single space around them. His frown only seemed to deepen the closer they got to Thompson land.

"You sure she wasn't the one shooting at us?" Henry asked, his voice low enough and close enough only she could hear.

And she should not have a bodily reaction to that, but she *did*. Annoyingly. "Sure? No. I'm not sure about anything." *Anything.*

He nodded. "Well, we'll get to the bottom of it back at the ranch."

"Are you sure you want to take her there?"

"Six military men against one question mark? Yeah, I'm sure."

"Six…" She looked up at him and he had an odd expression on his face like he wasn't supposed to say that. "You're *all* former military?"

"Runs in the family," he muttered. "Like apparently looks do in yours," he said, pointing to Quinn, who seemed as relaxed as anyone taking a casual stroll.

Quinn hadn't confirmed that they were sisters. She hadn't even fully confirmed she was a Peterson, but Jessie didn't know any other reason for looking that much alike. It was so strange. To watch someone who looked so much like her move and speak differently. To *be* a different person.

"Is there a way to give your brothers some kind of heads-up?"

"Already sent a text. It'll go through once we're in range."

"And then what?"

"Then we figure out what your twin is up to."

Chapter Ten

Henry kept the gun trained on this Quinn woman's back as they walked. He kept waiting for an ambush. A surprise. But nothing happened. Something was off, and it was irritating the hell out of him he couldn't pick up on what.

They crossed the fence line back to Thompson property. His brothers should have gotten his text by now and were hopefully all reconvening at the house like he'd asked.

He gave a quick glance back at Jessie and Sarabeth.

They were both fading. Shadows under their eyes, feet dragging a little. Jessie had Sarabeth's hand clutched in hers and somehow that made something clutch inside him. They were both too stubborn for their own good. They needed a tender, for heaven's sake. Well, they'd get tended at the ranch. Not by him, of course. Hazeleigh or Kate or somebody'd probably flutter about them.

Frustrated with his line of thinking, Henry turned his attention back to Quinn. Presumably Peterson. She looked exactly like Jessie, but it was easy enough to tell them apart when they moved. Jessie was all efficient movements, most of them designed to keep attention *off* her. Quinn moved with a certain kind of swagger, like she was used to wading into the center of attention.

Which made the space between his shoulder blades itch. She didn't need help. She didn't need to escape whatever she'd been a part of. So why was she acting like she did?

He scanned the horizon again. He kept waiting for someone—something—because this Quinn woman was *not* on the up and up.

But the stables to his own ranch came into view. He could see Landon cleaning a horse—but not in the normal spot they brushed and washed down the horses. He was the lookout. He'd send the message on to the other brothers that they were here.

Henry hadn't been lying when he'd told Jessie, stupidly, that he trusted his military brothers to take care of whatever threat this Quinn woman posed. They could handle whatever nonsense was going on about gold—or anything else.

What he worried about more, again stupidly, was how it would affect Jessie and Sarabeth. Whatever *it* was. Because this wasn't just weird obsessions with gold anymore. It was a twin sister—surely they had to be sisters, no matter how few questions Quinn had answered.

Family junk, and boy, he knew about some family junk.

They reached Landon and he didn't say anything, just moved to stand next to Henry while he told Quinn to keep walking to the house.

"So. This is a turn of events." He looked over his

shoulder. "You could stop running away at *any* point, kiddo."

Sarabeth wrinkled her nose at him.

"Hazeleigh coming back?" Henry asked.

"Yeah. She locked up back at the apartment. Listen." Landon lowered his voice, so only Henry could hear. "She said a truck drove by a couple times this morning. Never stopped. Never slowed. Non-descript enough she normally wouldn't have thought anything of it, but knowing Jessie was worried about going to the cops, Hazeleigh figured it was worth noting."

Henry did not like that. At all. "For sure. She get a plate?"

"Yeah, she's got it in her phone. I'll search it once I get to my computer, but I was out on my horse looking around when you texted. From where I was looking around the house, there's definitely someone camped out at the Peterson place, but I didn't want to get too close until we knew more."

"Get an idea of how many?"

"Not exactly, but definitely a small group. They weren't being too careful either. Footprints. Tents. Cal says ten at the most, three at the least."

That was still a broad range of people. He studied Quinn's back. "You think she was one of them?"

Landon joined his study. "Could be. Problem is I saw the evidence of people, but no actual people. Jake and Zara were up on the other side. Maybe they saw something else."

They reached the front porch and the door opened.

Cal stood there. Looking disapproving as always. "I guess we're doing this inside?"

"Sarabeth and Jessie need some food, water and rest."

"I wouldn't mind a little of that," Quinn said, and he could tell by the way Cal's expression hardened that she was grinning at him.

Henry decided to ignore her. "She doesn't have any other weapons. I searched her."

"Was it good for you too?" she asked with a smirk over her shoulder.

He didn't find her brand of humor very funny. Particularly in front of Sarabeth. *Yeah, that's who you're worried about.*

"Go on in and sit on the couch, Quinn."

"The hospitality is overwhelming." But she did as she was told. Of course, he had a gun, and while he wouldn't shoot her—he could likely take her down without use of the gun—she didn't need to know that.

"You guys keep an eye on her. I'm going to get Jessie and Sarabeth settled."

"You don't have to—"

"Come on now," he said over Jessie's argument. He handed Quinn's shotgun to Cal and then strode for the stairway, and was gratified when Sarabeth followed him, because it gave Jessie no other choice but to follow as well.

He led them up to his room. It just seemed the most reasonable option. He had a big bed they could share. It was across from the bathroom where they could clean themselves up.

He refused to look any further into it. He stepped into the room, and in a quick movement took his gun off his dresser and stuffed it into the back of his pants. He made sure his sweatshirt covered it as Jessie and Sarabeth stepped inside.

"Make yourselves comfortable. I'll have somebody bring you up something to eat, and one of the women to get you guys some clothes and towels and stuff so you can take a shower."

"You're just going to question this woman who's identical to me without me being in the room?" Jessie asked.

"You've had a rough night. Take a rest."

"No. Sarabeth can take a rest and I—"

"Mom, you said we were a team," Sarabeth interrupted.

Jessie's mouth firmed. "Sarabeth, we *are*, but you've been up all night. I have only been up half the night. And—"

"Take a rest, Jessie. I promise if we get anything out of her—which I'm not so sure we will—I will tell you all about it. And you'll be in a much better frame of mind to wade through whatever information we get if you've eaten something and taken a nap. I know you're probably not used to someone taking care of things, but you're going to have to deal."

She looked stricken enough he figured he hit the nail on the head there. She felt like she had to handle everything, and that was honorable enough. Probably even a necessity for most of her life, but in the here and now there was a whole group of people ready to take care of some things.

Kate appeared with a tray of food. "Hey, I bet you guys are hungry."

Sarabeth practically leaped for the food, and Henry took the distraction to slip away. Because he was going to get to the bottom of this Quinn woman and make sure she didn't pose a threat to Jessie or Sarabeth.

JESSIE DIDN'T KNOW what to do. She was being *fussed* over. By Hazeleigh and Kate. They brought food. Clothes. They practically forced her into the shower after Sarabeth's bath. And when she got out of the shower, with plans to check to make sure Sarabeth was asleep and then go downstairs to confront Quinn herself, Zara was waiting for her.

"Sarabeth is asleep, but Henry's got a big bed. You can crawl in there with her to catch a few hours."

Henry's bed. Oh, dear.

"I don't—"

"So far all that Quinn woman has done is flirt outrageously with all six men. She's not cracking, at least not for a while. Get some sleep. I know it feels like the guys are sweeping in and taking over, but I promise, they might try, but we women are on your side. And they can't stand up to us."

"Even Henry?" Jessie asked dubiously.

Zara seemed to consider. "Believe it or not, I think Henry's got quite the soft spot for Sarabeth." Then she tilted her head. "Well, or you."

"I'm sure it's Sarabeth," Jessie replied, trying to ignore…everything about how any of this made her feel. What did it matter? This was about what was going on. Not Henry and his soft spots. "She does have that kind of effect."

Zara shrugged. "Suit yourself. Just take care of yourself a little bit. I promise you won't miss a thing."

Jessie didn't know why she believed Zara. After all, they weren't friends. Zara was engaged to one of Henry's brothers. She had no reason to keep Jessie up-to-date on anything.

But God, Jessie was tired, and when Zara gently nudged her into the room and closed the door in her face, Jessie turned to see Sarabeth curled up on the bed. Fast asleep.

She didn't even remember sliding into bed next to Sarabeth.

But what felt like moments later, she opened her eyes, curled up in a ball in Henry's bed. The room around her was dark.

And Sarabeth was gone.

Please not again.

Jessie jumped from the bed and rushed to the door, but a Post-it on the doorknob stopped her. She pulled her hand back and held the now crumpled piece of paper up to the shaft of moonlight slanting through the window.

You were out cold. SB down with us.

She knew anyone in the house could have written it, but something about the nearly illegible masculine handwriting made her think it was Henry.

She didn't understand her reaction to him. Oh sure, she was mature enough to admit he was *attractive*. That the flutters could be boiled down to simple physical attraction. It meant no more or less than watching a movie with a good-looking actor in it.

What complicated things was the way he handled her daughter—not perfectly, but honestly. There was the way he'd said *because help is what we do*—and then proceeded to prove that, over and over again.

What was she supposed to do with *that*?

Jessie took a deep breath and settled herself. Henry might be involved in everything that was going on—somehow, someway—but he wasn't her primary concern. Sarabeth was. The mysterious Quinn was.

But she still checked her reflection in the bathroom mirror before she headed downstairs. Because she'd gone to bed with wet hair and no one needed to see the disaster it had become. She pulled it back as best she could with a rubber band she'd found underneath the sink. It didn't need to look good, it just needed to not look like Medusa.

Satisfied—well, not really, more like resigned—she went downstairs to find her daughter. The house was old but had been kept up well. There was some peeling paint here, or chipped baseboards there, but the wood was lovingly polished. Windows were scrubbed clean to let in the moonlight and starlight tonight—sun during the day.

It was nice. Homey.

And her heart stopped in her chest when she turned from the end of the stairs to enter the living room.

Henry and Sarabeth were facing each other, Sarabeth sitting on the floor, Henry lying on his side, a chessboard between them. Sarabeth was giggling like a loon, and Henry was grinning at her—somehow looking both big and imposing and perfectly comfortable sprawled out on the floor.

Her heartbeat started again, but the throbbing inside her chest was anything but calm or regular.

Oh dear.

Henry's eyes lifted, meeting her own. If he understood the look on her face—some mix of startled panic and a mushy feeling that did *not* belong in this scenario—he didn't act like it.

Thank *God.*

Though that easy-going grin that she'd never once seen on his face seemed to…tense. Firm. Still a smile, but not the same warmth.

She should *not* feel disappointment at that.

"I'm beating Henry at chess," Sarabeth announced.

"You can't beat someone at chess until you've won," Henry replied.

Jessie had to clear her throat to speak calmly and clearly. "When did you learn how to play chess?"

"Just now," Sarabeth replied, frowning at the board. "I was bored so Henry told me he'd teach me."

"That was very kind."

Henry shrugged and said nothing.

Jessie didn't know why she felt *nervous*, except she was in a strange house doing… Wait. Where was Quinn? "Where—"

A little cheer went up from the kitchen area and Jessie shifted so she could see. Quinn was in there with Cal and Dunne and Landon and they appeared to be doing…shots.

"What on earth."

"She challenged Cal to a drinking contest," Henry said, moving a piece on the chessboard after Sarabeth did. "For some inexplicable reason, Cal agreed to it."

"With the strange woman we know nothing about?"

"Don't worry. Dunne's playing guard."

"I feel like I've woken up in an alternate reality. What time is it?"

"Nine."

"Well, thank you for everything. Really, I don't even know how to express my gratitude, but Sarabeth and I should be getting out of your way and getting home."

Henry got to his feet, a strangely graceful movement for such a big man. Like some sort of predatory cat. "I'm afraid that's not going to be an option just yet," he said in that closed off, foreboding way that irritated her even before the words penetrated.

Jessie frowned at him. "What?"

He looked down at Sarabeth, then up at Jessie again. She could tell he wanted to say something, but not in front of Sarabeth. Jessie could send Sarabeth to her— Henry's, someone's—room, but that would only pique Sarabeth's curiosity. Besides, they needed to go *home*.

Someone swept in. It wasn't Hazeleigh or Zara, so it had to be the other woman. Kate, Jessie thought. They'd been in a class together in elementary school…maybe. She couldn't quite remember.

"Hey, guys. I'm going to feed the barn kittens we've

got out on the summer porch. I thought you might want to help, Sarabeth."

Sarabeth's eyes widened. "Kittens?"

Kate nodded. "They're all holed up underneath the porch furniture, but they'll come out and play if we bring them some cream."

Sarabeth looked up at Jessie. It was a distraction, and it would allow Henry to talk freely. Jessie managed a smile and nodded. "Sure."

Sarabeth scrambled after Kate. She wore an adult size T-shirt that went down to her calves. It was definitely a man's shirt and Jessie felt something very strange over her daughter possibly wearing one of Henry's T-shirts.

When he put his hand on her elbow she nearly jumped a foot. "Let's talk on the front porch."

"Right. Sure. Yes." She felt like she'd been electrocuted. Surely the way-too-long nap she'd taken had dulled her senses. Some fresh air would help. She needed to get her brain in gear.

She stepped out into the cool summer evening. The stars and moon were shining, most of the world dark except the last hints of day to the western horizon. It was beautiful out here.

And her life was a mess.

"I figured telling Sarabeth to scram wasn't the way to be able to talk to you alone. I texted Kate once you were up," Henry said. He stood, leaning against the porch post, studying her.

Jessie's heart jangled in her chest. "That's very…perceptive."

"Yeah, well, listen, when Hazeleigh was at your place in case Sarabeth came back, she saw someone casing the place."

"Casing?"

"Driving past. Looking for something. Someone's looking for you guys, Jessie."

It wasn't a surprise. Not now. Not after being shot at and finding a woman who looked just like her. Nothing was a surprise. "Henry, I don't think this is just about the gold anymore."

"No, it seems unlikely."

"But I genuinely don't know *what* it's about."

Henry nodded. He was just a dark shadow out here, and it should make her nervous. He should look scary and dangerous, like a ghost. But she found his presence, his calm demeanor, reassuring.

Whatever this was, they'd figure out how to handle it.

They? Since when were you ever a they *beyond Sarabeth? You need to figure this out on your own.*

"I realize people looking for us is a problem." God, it was a problem. "But Sarabeth and I can't just…stay here. If someone really is looking for me, they'll find me. At the apartment. Here." She thought about Quinn, her identical *twin*. "Maybe they already have."

"Well, until we figure that out, you should stay here."

She narrowed her eyes at him, because that wasn't an invitation. "Should or will?"

Henry seemed to mull that over. "I get the feeling telling you what to do would go over about as well as telling Sarabeth what to do."

"So you're going to pretend like there's a choice, even though you don't plan on giving me one?"

"I told you a while back, I'm not letting anything happen to you two. So no, there's no choice. The smart, sensible thing is to stay here till we sort out Quinn and whatever else is going on."

"I have a job," Jessie said, feeling tears sting her eyes. Because she knew she was safer here than in town, but that didn't mean she and Sarabeth were completely safe. It just meant she had to leave. No Wilde roots for Sarabeth. Maybe they should go back to Florida. Or somewhere new. Iowa or Kansas. Disappear, the way she'd done once before. "Sarabeth starts school in a few weeks." She'd have to get somewhere she could safely enroll her. "You have a full house as it is. We can't just…"

"That gives us a few weeks then, doesn't it? And if you can't take time off work, that's fine. One of us will just go with you. We don't know what's going on, so no, we can't just hide here and hope it all goes away. But that doesn't mean I'm about to let you go gallivanting around waiting to get kidnapped again."

"Gallivanting?" Temper spurted, and she recognized it as something not *only* because of his high-handed, obnoxious attitude, but boy, was it a nice place to land.

"I'm trying to put things nicely, but it's not my forte."

She snorted. "No kidding." But she supposed beneath the anger she appreciated the fact if nothing else she wasn't getting any lies from Henry. "Don't be nice. Just be honest."

"That I can promise."

"Henry, we can't stay. You have to know that."

There was a long, fraught silence where he was only a shadow. A disapproving one. Then he stepped forward, into the little swath of moonlight. Too close— and she was too stubborn to back away.

Or too caught up in the way the moonlight softened that hard face and hardened those soft eyes.

"So you're going to run?"

"I *have* to run. I told you it's all I'm any good at."

"You could face it. Get to the bottom of it. We're going to help you, Jessie. Why would you run away from that?"

"You don't owe us anything. I know you have some warped guilt over what happened with your mother—"

"Excuse *me*?" he said, deadly calm dripping from both words. The kind of deadly calm that made a smart woman shut up and rethink.

"You don't think I understand? I know you don't talk much, and you rarely speak kindly when you do, but I can read between the lines. Your mother died, and you felt responsible. You joined the army—or whatever military branch—to assuage your guilt. It didn't work, so you got out. You and your brothers started this, away from war or whatever horrible things you must have seen. But you're still out here, helping whoever you can, trying to make that guilt go away. How right am I?"

His face was inscrutable. "Maybe fifty percent. Tops."

"But the fifty percent is the fifty percent that matters, isn't it? I don't want your parental guilt."

"Even if it meant Sarabeth could stay here, where

you know she wants to stay? Be safe. Put down roots. Getting to the bottom of it means you could give her what I know you want to give her—because you might argue with me or fake skittishness with me, but I can read between the lines, too, Jessie. You wanted to build a life for her here. Why would you give up on that so easily? When help is being offered."

It hurt. In so many little ways she couldn't catalog them all. Of course she wanted to give Sarabeth all those things. But… "I was offered help once. To get out. To escape. But it was just a slightly different version of the same prison."

"This isn't escape. And it isn't prison. Trust me. I've got no use caging you or your little girl. I'm offering you a solution."

"I don't know if I can believe that." But God, she wanted to. She wanted to give in and hand it over to him. To believe these people she barely knew would sweep in and find a *solution*. So she could give Sarabeth everything he'd outlined.

She didn't want to run again. The very thought filled her with exhaustion and dread. She wanted to lean, just a little. And Henry, so big and sturdy and certain, seemed a perfectly safe place to lean.

He even stepped a little closer, close enough it wouldn't take much at all to rest her cheek on his chest. But she stopped herself. Looked up at him instead.

"I know you don't have any reason to trust me, or any of us really. But why don't you give us a chance? Running is always an answer if you figure you don't like how it's going. For now you don't even have to trust me. You just have to stay put."

But the problem was she did trust him. Far too much.

Chapter Eleven

Jessie looked like a silvery Western fairy out in the moonlight, and Henry realized far too late that standing this close...posed a problem. He could smell her shampoo, and it didn't matter that it had to be the same one Kate or Zara used. On her it smelled different. Enticing.

In the dark everything about her seemed soft. Oh, even now he knew it hid an inner strength she kept well covered, but her hair looked like it would feel like velvet if he reached out and ran his fingers through it.

And why the hell was he thinking about touching her hair?

He might have stepped back. For very inexplicable reasons he felt scalded, but he knew enough to realize if he broke the moment she'd run now. When she needed to stay put. Running would only put her and Sarabeth in continued danger.

He needed... No. This wasn't about what he needed. It was about what was smart. She wanted to run? He wouldn't stop her. But if she could suck it up and stay, they could get to the bottom of it. So they could both stay put. Both build a life he knew they each so desperately wanted.

She could run. He could let her. But it would be smarter to stay.

He had to curl his hands into fists at the thought of actually letting her run. It made him want to grab her in the here and now. Shake some sense into her. Or something else. Something far more dangerous. Because who was he kidding?

If she tried to run, he'd stop her in a heartbeat.

Over and over. He didn't know why. Didn't want to analyze why. It was the right thing to do and a long time ago he'd promised himself he'd always do the right thing. Even if it was hard. Even if it hurt.

Why did all of this crawl inside him and *hurt*, when neither Jessie nor Sarabeth should mean anything to him?

Should being the operative word.

She inhaled a long, shaky breath even as her eyes continued to hold his. He should back off. Away. *Now*.

The door opened. Henry held himself very still. He wasn't about to let anyone make this look like more than it was. No matter how close he was currently standing to Jessie.

Who jumped like a rabbit caught in a predator's clutches.

Henry flicked what he hoped was a cool, unfeeling glance at Dunne standing there in the doorway.

"Said she's ready to talk."

Henry nodded. "We'll be in in a minute."

Dunne nodded. Said nothing. His expression gave

nothing away. And *still*, Henry stiffened. He looked down at the woman who had him tied up in knots. He should go inside.

But he couldn't quite help himself.

"Don't run, Jessie. Please." Then he stepped inside where he could leave all that…weird, uncomfortable emotion outside.

Quinn, looking identical to Jessie down to the way the stray hair from her band seemed to curl around her face, helped ice it out.

He didn't trust this woman, and no matter how much she looked like Jessie, there was a cold, calculating glint to her eyes. And he didn't like her here.

But here she was. While the living room was mostly empty, his brothers were spread out around the house strategically. Cal still at the kitchen table—likely not as inebriated as he pretended to be when he was having a drinking contest with the woman.

Dunne at the entrance to the kitchen taking his job as guard seriously. Henry couldn't see the rest of them, but no doubt Brody was out with Kate and Sarabeth and the kittens. Jake guarding the back door so they didn't come in without warning. Landon, hopefully, on his computer trying to come up with something on Quinn or the truck that was driving by Jessie's apartment.

"So?"

She shrugged. "So what?"

"What have you got to say?" Henry replied.

"What do you want to know?"

Henry struggled not to groan. "Who are you? Why

are you here? Who are you here with? Who's casing Jessie and Sarabeth's place?"

The last question seemed to surprise her. There was just the slightest flicker in her expression, like she had to rethink some things.

"Let's start with who you are," Jessie said. She'd quietly followed him in. And whatever breathy uncertainty had been on display outside was gone.

It gave Henry the uncomfortable realization that he shouldn't lead this questioning. That Jessie needed to wade in there and ask her own questions, handle this as much as she could. For her own peace of mind.

It was hard—way too hard—to step back. To give Jessie the floor.

But he knew he had to.

Jessie swallowed as Henry stepped back. At first, she thought he was going to take over, or worse, leave her alone to handle it.

But he did neither. He simply gave her the space to face off against this identical woman. Stayed close, right next to her really, but made it clear she…was in charge for the time being.

He hadn't just told her to stay. He'd said *please*.

But that was not what was important right now. Getting to the bottom of her mysterious twin was.

"Who are you and why do we look so much alike?"

Quinn shrugged. "We've got the same parents."

"We're twins?"

"I mean, I assume. It's not like I remember you when

we were fetuses. I didn't exactly know I had an identical twin out there looking just like me."

"The word *exactly* makes me think you had more of an idea than Jessie did."

Quinn flicked a glance at Henry and considered. "Yeah, looks like. I always knew I had a sister, and that my mom had decided to take her when she left."

Left. But that wasn't right. "My mother died in childbirth."

Quinn seemed unfazed by that. "Not the story I got."

"But it makes more sense. That she would have died, complications to having twins, than that she just took one of us."

"Maybe she could only get away with one of us."

That had an uncomfortable pit of…sadness…grow in Jessie's gut. She couldn't imagine having to leave a daughter behind, but she also knew how desperate she had once been to escape that compound. A compound… Quinn should have been at. "But I lived at my father's compound for over five years. I never saw you. No one ever mentioned you."

"Yeah, for a reason. *Obviously.*"

"How is any of this obvious?"

"I really don't get how you could have been a part of it for five years and not picked up on any of it, but okay, let's lay it all on the table here. You don't know about the person who looks just like you? It's because one of you is meant to replace the other."

"Explain," Henry ordered, in that voice that likely would have prompted her to fall all over herself to explain if he'd been talking to her.

But he wasn't, so she could probably stop *fluttering* over that dark, intimidating way he'd said that one word.

"Look, I'm not a part of it," Quinn said, spreading her hands wide. "Whatever dear old Dad's got going on is always his business. I'm a pawn. You're probably a pawn. I don't know for what. Gold, sure, but there's more now that Rob's dead. Dad knows I'm a bit of a flight risk, and not totally on his side, my bad, but I'm willing to wager he thinks the kid knows something."

Jessie's entire body went cold. "Knows something?"

"About the gold. Again, *obviously*."

None of this seemed obvious to Jessie, and the idea Sarabeth was on her father's radar was…beyond terrifying. The cold froze her. She had no words. No thoughts. Just *fear*.

And then she felt a hand on her back. Warm and firm.

"But it's more than the gold," Henry said. His tone was low and controlled like maybe the world wasn't ending. "If anything is obvious, it's that."

Quinn tilted her head, seemed to study the space between Jessie and Henry—what little there was of it, because he'd come closer. Put his hand on her back. A reassuring gesture that something…something could be done to protect Sarabeth. Had to be done.

"Got yourself quite the bodyguard. Not bad." Quinn looked over at Dunne in the doorway between kitchen and living room. "Or should I say bodyguard*s*. Must be nice."

"Nothing about this is nice." Because her daughter might be in danger. Because Henry thought she should stay and fight and Jessie felt like all these unanswered questions only added up to one thing: run.

Quinn got to her feet. "You know what? Let's cut the crap, huh?" She moved past Henry and Jessie and walked over to where Dunne was blocking the way to the kitchen. She swayed a little, like she wasn't steady on her feet. "Move, would ya?"

He looked over his shoulder at Cal, and decidedly didn't move.

"That's real cute." She looked back at Henry. "You guys are a real band of brothers, huh? And you!" She pointed to Cal over Dunne's shoulder. "You're the leader. So why don't you tell your little soldier to move the hell out of my way?"

"Pass," Cal replied dispassionately.

She pushed at Dunne's chest. Dunne rolled his eyes. "You're not half as drunk as you'd like me to believe."

And then Jessie watched the way the act all fell away. No more stumbles. No more vaguely slurred words. Quinn's eyes, the same exact shade as Jessie's own, narrowed. She reached out to punch him, but it was a fake. When Dunne grabbed that hand to stop the blow, shifted his weight away from her lifted knee, she used her other hand to punch his leg.

Jessie knew Dunne limped, and by the way the blow landed on an awkward part of his leg, she figured Quinn had deduced where the injury was and hit exactly that spot. Because Dunne let out a whiff of breath and she pushed by him.

Jessie hurried after her, Henry right behind her. But

Cal stopped Quinn before she got much farther than the kitchen table, not that it mattered.

"Hey, kid?" Quinn yelled in the direction of the screen door. Sarabeth was with Kate and some kittens on the other side of that screen. "When are you going to tell your mom what you know?"

SARABETH PRETENDED LIKE she didn't hear the lady who looked like Mom but had…something different. It wasn't looking at her that Sarabeth felt it. It was when she talked. It was something…uncomfortable.

She let Kate distract her with a cat, as the adults scuffled and argued inside. After a few minutes, Zara suggested they go upstairs. When Sarabeth had asked to take one of the kittens, Zara and Kate had looked at each other with matching eyes of worry and uncertainty.

But they'd let her take the kitten as they'd gone with her back to the bedroom upstairs. In the kitchen, she didn't see anyone. All the way upstairs she didn't see or hear anyone.

Her heart beat hard against her chest. But no one asked her what she knew. No one poked at her. They left her alone in the room.

She held on to the cat for dear life, and then curled up on the big bed. She rested her chin on the headboard and looked out at the window it was shoved underneath.

Things were bad. She'd thought coming to the Thompson Ranch would mean they were safe, but the lady who looked like Mom wasn't safe. Sarabeth wasn't sure she was *bad*, but she wasn't good.

Get up to 4
FREE FABULOUS BOOKS
in your welcome box!

To thank you for being a loyal reader we'd like to send you up to 4 FREE BOOKS, absolutely free when you try the Harlequin Reader Service.

Just write "YES" on the Loyal Reader Voucher and we'll send you your welcome box with 2 free books from each series you choose plus free mystery gifts! Each welcome box is worth over $20.

Try **Harlequin® Romantic Suspense** and get 2 books featuring heart-racing page-turners with unexpected plot twists and irresistible chemistry that will keep you guessing to the very end.

Try **Harlequin Intrigue® Larger-Print** 2 books featuring action-packed stories that will keep you on the edge of your seat. Solve the crime and deliver justice at all costs.

Or **TRY BOTH** and get 2 books from each series!

Your welcome box is completely free, even the shipping! If you continue with your subscription, you can look forward to curated monthly shipments of brand-new books from your selected series, always at a discount off the cover price! Plus you can cancel any time.

So don't miss out, return your Loyal Readers Voucher today to get your Free Welcome Box.

Pam Powers

LOYAL READER
FREE BOOKS VOUCHER
WELCOME BOX

YES! I Love Reading, please send me a welcome box with up to 4 FREE BOOKS and Free Mystery Gifts from the series I select.

Just write in "YES" on the dotted line below then return this card today and we'll send your welcome box asap!

➡ YES ⬅
- - - - - - -

Which do you prefer?

☐ **Harlequin® Romantic Suspense**
240/340 HDL GRTY

☐ **Harlequin Intrigue® Larger-Print**
199/399 HDL GRTY

☐ **BOTH**
240/340 & 199/399
HDL GQ93

FIRST NAME	LAST NAME

ADDRESS

APT.#	CITY

STATE/PROV.	ZIP/POSTAL CODE

EMAIL ☐ Please check this box if you would like to receive newsletters and promotional emails from Harlequin Enterprises ULC and its affiliates. You can unsubscribe anytime.

HI/HRS-622-LR_LRV22

When the door squeaked open, Sarabeth assumed it would be Mom. Coming to ask her what she was hiding.

But it was Henry.

Sarabeth held the cat tighter. She wasn't scared of Henry, but something about his expression made her stomach cramp into knots. "Where's Mom?"

"Hazeleigh convinced her to sit down and eat something before she came to bed, so I said I'd come check on you."

"I'm okay. Can I name your cat?"

"Not my cat."

"I think he looks like a Henry."

"I think *she* looks like a Henrietta."

"Oh." Sarabeth thought the cat looked like a boy, but she hadn't checked to make sure her feelings were accurate.

"Sarabeth."

She didn't like the way he said her name. It came out like…like Mom. Like she was both in trouble but not in trouble. Like she did something wrong, but she wasn't going to get punished. She was just going to feel yucky about it. So she didn't look at him. She looked at the little black fuzzball squirming in her arms.

She felt the bed dip a little, and she had to look over at Henry. He'd sat down on the bed, but on the very edge of the other side. His eyes were on her. He didn't look mad or mean or that confused way he'd looked when she'd cried. He looked like…

She'd thought about what it would be like to have a father. She'd had dreams of what he might be like—

not her real, biological one, but someone who wanted to be her *dad*.

Lately, they tended to all look and sound like Henry.

"Why would you keep something from her?" he asked. Soft, almost hurt, not the usual grumpiness or meanness she'd wanted. Nothing she could fight against.

Sarabeth stared hard out the window. Outside everything was dark or silver. Shadows or moonlight. Tears threatened, but she wasn't about to cry in front of Henry again. He hadn't handled it *so* badly, and at least she hadn't upset him like she did when she cried in front of Mom, but still. Mom always said a woman had her pride, and Sarabeth supposed this was hers.

"I'm not really keeping anything from Mom. I mean, she doesn't know about the gold coin I have."

"Does someone else?"

"No!"

"Then why do you look guilty?"

Sarabeth frowned down at Henrietta—Henry might have said that as a joke, but she liked it. So there. She wasn't guilty. She wasn't keeping anything from anyone.

Mostly.

But why would that lady know… Why would that lady…

"Sarabeth." And again, Henry's voice was gentle. Not that gruff ordering thing he did so often. "You've got something in that brain of yours none of us have. Maybe you're scared, or you don't want to get in trouble, or whatever. I get it, but honey, you've got to be honest with me, at the very least. What are we missing?"

Sarabeth swallowed at the lump in her throat. She didn't know what to do with him calling her *honey*. She wanted to crawl into his lap, cry on his shoulder and pretend he was her dad and would take care of everything.

But he wasn't. She'd killed her father. She'd taken care of things.

Or thought she had.

Which was so much of why she hadn't wanted to tell Mom. She thought she'd handle it herself. Save Mom the worry, and maybe, Sarabeth had wanted to stay in Wilde more than she'd cared about being safe.

"Mom will want to go away if I tell you," she managed in a croaky whisper. "I don't want to leave Wilde. I like it here."

Henry thought that over for a moment, the kind of pause where she knew an adult was actually listening to her. Not just trying to figure out a way to get what they wanted.

"You might be right. Your mom wants to protect you more than anything, but I know if she felt safe here, she'd want to stay here. Why don't you tell me, and I can make sure it's safe for you guys to stay here."

She looked up at him, studied his face. He had nice eyes. No matter what he was doing—even when he was yelling or swearing—he had nice eyes, and he'd never even acted like he *might* hit her. Henry had always done exactly what he'd said he'd do, and he was always gentle with her and Mom, even when he was mean.

She believed he *could* make it safe for them here, but

she also knew he wasn't in charge of where she went. Mom was. Which meant…she needed more than *could*.

"Do you promise?"

Henry's eyebrows drew together and he continued to study her as Henrietta escaped her grasp and tried to take a leap off the bed. Henry caught her easily, then handed her back to Sarabeth.

"I promise," he said as he passed the cat back to her.

He held her gaze when he said it, and he sounded like…he didn't really want to promise. She knew from experience with Mom that was usually when she was the best at keeping promises. Because if she broke one she made even though she didn't want to, she'd feel extra guilty.

Sarabeth didn't understand that part of adults, but whatever worked.

So she told him. She wasn't sure it was what that Quinn lady meant, or even what Henry expected, but it was the only thing she knew.

"When… Rob had my mom tied up, and he let me go… It was because I was small and could crawl into some spaces he wanted to look for the gold."

"Okay."

"He had it all planned out. For me. And when it wasn't where he thought, when I didn't get him what he wanted, he didn't have any use for me."

Henry got very, very still. She wasn't sure he took a breath. "He wanted you. Not her."

Sarabeth chewed on her bottom lip. "I don't know that," she replied. Because it wasn't like Rob had said it.

It wasn't like anyone had ever come out and said she'd been the real target of Rob taking them.

It was just…a feeling she'd gotten. There was something about *her* Rob had focused on in the beginning of all that horrible stuff. And at first she'd thought…

Sarabeth had to fight back the tears again, because it was embarrassing and awful and bad. She knew it was bad. Mom had been taken and tied up and she shouldn't have hoped that her father wanted something to do with *her*. She should have just hated him.

But she hadn't. And she couldn't ever tell Mom that. She couldn't tell anyone that.

She felt the bed move, and then Henry came to sit next to her. He put his hand on her back, rubbed up and down once. Just like she'd told him to do back when she'd cried the first time.

"Let it out, kid. You'll feel better."

She didn't want to—let it out *or* feel better—but she couldn't swallow down the lump or blink back the tears when he was rubbing her back like Mom did when she was upset. She couldn't fight it back when she knew she was the bad guy and nobody understood.

She didn't want anybody to understand.

But that only made the tears fall, her breathing hitch. And she couldn't seem to do anything else but what he said—let it out. She pressed her forehead into his shoulder and cried while he rubbed her back and told her it would be okay.

Chapter Twelve

When Jessie finally stepped into *Henry's* room, which she preferred to think of as *the room they were staying in*, she expected to find Sarabeth curled up in bed. Hopefully asleep. Maybe someone in the room with her, watching her, but certainly not her daughter crying on a big man's shoulder while he rubbed a hand up and down her back.

She could tell Henry wasn't comfortable by the grimace on his face, but he soothed Sarabeth anyway.

Jessie just froze there in the doorway. While her daughter cried, and Henry handled it. She knew she should have rushed forward, but she couldn't seem to get her feet to work.

Surely it was natural for any woman to feel a little fluttery over a guy who was good with her daughter... when said guy looked like *that*. It certainly didn't mean she was developing actual feelings for him. She was smarter than that.

She really needed to be smarter than that.

Henry turned as if he sensed her there. Their gazes met. She let out a shaky breath, needing to get a handle on herself. On everything.

He gave her a kind of *please, God, take over* look and she stepped into the room, still feeling far too shaky for her own good.

But with an ease that felt more like years of partnership than a few days, Henry exchanged places with her and she wrapped her arms around Sarabeth. "Baby. What's wrong?"

Sarabeth shook her head and burrowed in deeper. Jessie soothed, sang an old lullaby she rarely got to pull out these days because Sarabeth usually rolled her eyes and said she was too old for baby stuff. But she let her sing. Let her tuck her into bed.

And when Sarabeth slid off to sleep in just a few minutes, when usually she tossed and turned and fought sleep with everything she was, Jessie knew she was exhausted. Hopefully that was an explanation for the uncharacteristic crying.

Yes, not at all killing her father, running away and now dealing with a mysterious twin sister for her mother.

Jessie squeezed her eyes shut for a moment, her hand still rubbing circles on Sarabeth's sleeping back. Guilt was trying to win, but Jessie knew guilt didn't solve problems. If she'd gotten Sarabeth into all these messes, it was only her job to stop the pattern. Fix the problem.

Maybe Henry had been right back there. She couldn't run. Running didn't work. Eventually everything you were running from caught up with you.

And her daughter was paying the price.

She felt something more than heard it and looked up.

Henry was still there. He was in the doorway, but she didn't get the impression he'd ever left. He'd just stood there. Watching. It wasn't exactly embarrassing. It was just…he'd watched a private moment.

Of course, she'd watched him comfort Sarabeth. But Sarabeth was *hers* and…

Maybe she was exhausted, too. Though she didn't feel it. She felt uneasy and revved and…other things that it didn't do to think about.

Henry jerked his chin toward the hallway. Jessie steeled herself for…whatever and got up and followed him outside. He left the door open, but he spoke quietly, as if he wasn't sure Sarabeth was really asleep.

"She knows more than she's letting on." Henry looked back at the room. "She feels guilty about something."

"Guilty?"

"I might not get the myriad of eleven-year-old girl feelings, but what I saw in there? Guilt. I'm sure of it. Not just about her father."

Jessie rubbed at her chest. Everything seemed to contract there, a hard, painful knot.

"Look, I can only take one crying person a day. It's like a rule."

She laughed, in spite of all that pressure and pain, and sure, guilt. "I'll do my best."

"I'm going to talk to Quinn. That woman *also* knows more than she's letting on, and I'd rather yell it out of a grown obnoxious woman than a little girl."

"I want to be there." She looked back into the darkened room. She didn't want to leave Sarabeth alone. It was silly. She was in a house full of people, and Jessie knew she'd made herself at home here.

"I can get someone to come sit with her."

Jessie chewed on her bottom lip. "I feel like I'm pawning her off."

"You can't have it all ways, Jess. No one can."

She wondered if he noticed he'd shortened her name. Then she wondered why *she'd* noticed. It certainly didn't matter. It was probably just faster.

What did matter, sadly, was that he was right. She couldn't have it all the ways. That was like the single mom motto. "Yeah, isn't that the truth. Can't have it all ways. Can't have it any good way."

Henry stood there, frowning at her. She was about to apologize—no one needed to listen to her pity party, her guilt, but before she could, he put his hand on her arm. Why did it have to be so *big*? So *warm*? Why did she have to feel settled by his fingers curling around her biceps?

"Surely you don't need me to tell you you're doing a good job."

"At what?"

"The whole mom thing," he said gruffly.

"Ha, well, it doesn't feel like it. My daughter is guilty and crying herself to sleep and running away and was forced to *kill* her father so he wouldn't kill anyone else."

His grip on her tightened, just a little. Just enough to have her gaze rising to his. And his dark eyes were solemn. Serious. Enough to have her heart shuddering in her chest.

"Jessie, trust me, bad moms don't care. They don't have guilt. They give up. On their kids. On themselves. They do *not* beat themselves up. They do *not* worry—at least not about the kid."

"Well." She had to clear her throat to say the rest. She wished it were emotion that was clogged there, but it was something else too, and it had to do with the way her body reacted when he touched her. She tried for a casual smile. "Who knew you could give a decent enough pep talk."

"Yeah, who knew," he muttered.

He didn't let go of her arm. He just stared at her with his eyebrows drawn together, and his *who knew* seemed to take on a different meaning. Like who knew there could be this? Who knew…?

His gaze dropped to her mouth, and her heart jumped. Just *jumped*. She was probably hallucinating, but…

THERE WERE TOO many things circling around in his brain. That was what Henry would blame this on. Too many thoughts. Too many feelings. Comforting Sarabeth had messed with him somehow. Messed with everything.

And now Jessie was standing here and he could see it on her face. The guilt and the worry and that little hitch of…clearly not feeling good enough. When he'd watched her. Hug her daughter, ease her into bed, sing songs and just shower her with love.

She hadn't demanded answers, and he knew she wanted them. She hadn't scolded or tried to do anything but *comfort*.

He couldn't stand the thought she might not know *that* was the mark of a mother. Care and comfort over her own wants. That she would let guilt and everything that had happened that wasn't Jessie's fault cloud the very basic fact she was a good mom. The best mom.

And it shouldn't feel *good* that she'd said he gave a good pep talk. It shouldn't feel *good*, her arm under his hands. Strong and tough, but still soft. He shouldn't want to or need to comfort her or touch her or talk to her.

He shouldn't notice her mouth, study it. He shouldn't want to...

He released her. Probably abruptly. "I'll go grab Landon or Hazeleigh." And then he escaped. Like a *coward*.

But what the hell was wrong with him anyway?

Thinking about kissing her in the middle of all this. He was an idiot. Warped. Yeah, he knew that. He'd always known that. Usually he left vulnerable moms and their good kids out of it.

Clearly there was something about helping a woman that made a guy think there was something romantic there when, *ha ha ha*, like romantic was something he'd ever been involved in. He wasn't Jake or Landon or even Brody. Somehow they'd turned these types of situations into something...

Domestic. Jake and Zara were getting married. Hazeleigh and Landon had settled into that little cabin and lived together like an old married couple. Brody and Kate took care of everyone in the house like they were the parents of the group.

All because they'd been thrown into some danger together. Like that just...forged some kind of bond. Like a few bullets flying made love sprout into existence.

He wished he didn't believe his brothers were in love, whatever that meant. But he saw them all. The way they were with each other. It wasn't all lovey-dovey looks and touches. It was arguments and makeups. It was casual gestures. The way Jake would slide his hand down Zara's ponytail—the way she'd waited on him when he'd been recovering from his gunshot wound when he was pretty sure Zara Hart waited on no one *ever*.

It was the way Brody and Kate made meals together like it was a dance, and Landon and Hazeleigh looked at each other with knowing smiles like they could read each other's thoughts.

And none of this had to do with him and Jessie because wanting to kiss her was just…basic chemistry. Liking the kid was just… She was a good kid. Watching Jessie sing and tuck Sarabeth into *his* bed in *his* room and feeling like…it was kind of nice. The kind of thing he wouldn't mind seeing over and over again.

He stopped at the bottom of the stairs and shook his head like a dog trying to shake off water from its fur.

This was *insane*. He had to get his head on straight. Because this was bad. This was lethal. Someone had shot at them. That Quinn woman—a near identical copy of Jessie—was nothing but trouble, clearly. Sarabeth was in *danger*.

That was what he needed to be thinking about.

Landon came around the corner, stopped and studied Henry. "You good?"

"Sure. Where's Quinn?"

"Oh, Dunne and Cal are keeping an eye on her in

Dunne's room. She doesn't act like she's going to bolt. I think she likes the attention."

"I think she's a damn threat."

"Maybe, but we can handle that, can't we?"

"Yeah. *We* can. Listen, Jessie and I are going to talk to Quinn. Jess wants someone up there with the kid. Sarabeth is asleep, but you know, just in case."

Landon nodded. "I'll do it."

"Great," Henry replied, feeling decidedly *not* great. Especially as Landon continued to study him.

"You're sure wrapped up in this."

Henry scowled. "So what? You think I'm following the danger-love pattern here? Because I don't think so." And he'd really proven his point bringing up *love* of all damn things.

"Well, truth be told, I kind of had a thing for Hazeleigh before all that danger. Jake for Zara, too. It wasn't like danger *led* to love. It was just the situation to act on already-there feelings, I guess."

Why did that not make him feel *any* better? He'd much rather blame all this…whatever on danger mixing stuff up. "I don't have feelings," Henry muttered.

"Oh, buddy, you got a whole boatload of them. You just don't know what to do with them." He gave Henry a hard slap on the back. "I'll send Jessie down." Then he disappeared up the stairs.

A boatload seemed like a conservative estimate right about now, particularly when Jessie came down the stairs in clothes that weren't her own. Her hair had dried curlier than it usually was after her shower.

"Have you slept at all? I slept the day away and didn't think to ask. You were up—"

"I'm fine," he replied. "Do I not look it?"

She stared at him and, oddly enough, a faint pink stained her cheeks. "Sure, you look fine."

Why did that make him want to smile? *Because you're warped, remember?* Right. "She's in Dunne's room. Follow me."

He led her through the house. Dunne had the biggest room—what had once been the parlor. It wasn't in the best of shape, but since Dunne did any necessary medical administering, he got the extra space. Besides, his injured leg made the stairs too hard for him.

Henry knocked once, then entered. Cal stood by the window, looking out into the dark with a scowl on his face. Dunne was stretched out on his bed reading a book. Quinn sat on a chair in the middle of the room, pretending to gaze at the ceiling.

Henry was pretty sure she was studying the men in the room with her, just as they were studying her without looking like it.

"Give us a few alone with her," Henry said.

Dunne looked at Cal, Cal at Henry. He nodded and they both left.

"Spooky, the six of you," Quinn said, pretending to shudder. "Like you can read each other's minds."

"Maybe we can," Henry replied.

Quinn grinned at him. "You don't seem like the type to believe in mind reading."

He didn't respond to that, just pulled another chair

over so Jessie could sit across from Quinn. So identical even *he* thought it was eerie.

Quinn studied them both—Jessie sitting, him standing behind her. There was a lot going on there, and Henry hated admitting he didn't know what. He *knew* she posed a threat—there had been gunshots, then her. She'd pointed a gun at Jessie. But she sure didn't act like she was going to run or hurt them.

Maybe she was waiting for backup. Henry considered it the most plausible possibility, but she also didn't act like she was waiting. So maybe it was far off. Maybe she was a good actor.

No matter what, though, whatever she was waiting for, whoever she was, she wasn't going to hurt Jessie and Sarabeth.

He was going to make sure of it.

Chapter Thirteen

Jessie couldn't stop studying Quinn, trying to find differences. But they were *so* identical. Sure, Jessie would never sit in a chair that way—all languid like she didn't have a care in the world. And yes, Jessie had a freckle on her earlobe that Quinn didn't have. But that seemed to be the only things: attitude and a *freckle*.

Who would notice that?

"So. Aren't you going to interrogate me?" Quinn asked, her gaze flicking from Henry to Jessie and then back to Henry again. She grinned at Henry with a kind of brash flirtatiousness Jessie could never imagine having herself.

Jessie frowned a little at that. It was clear it was all this kind of...bravado act, but Jessie didn't really like it being geared toward Henry. No matter how stupid that was—or how brick-wall-like he responded.

And hardly the point. Hardly important. Jessie sighed, overwhelmed. So many feelings. So many questions. "I don't even know where to begin."

"The beginning is a good place," Henry said firmly, making her glad he was here. She didn't want him to take the lead, per se. She just needed…someone to help her focus. "You're twin sisters. Identical twin sisters."

"I guess," Quinn said. "I mean, that's what I was always told. But I've been lied to a lot. Maybe it's a coincidence we look the same."

"Yes, that's *so* likely."

Quinn grinned.

But Jessie couldn't find the situation humorous. "How? How can we be identical twins? Are you telling me our mother *didn't* die in childbirth? That she had two identical babies and then took me to her mother and left you behind?"

"Don't really know. I don't remember her. The story I got was the ditched-me thing. They used that one pretty hard against me for a while, so died in childbirth seems just as likely. Though not sure how we would have been split up if so. Still, most stuff they tried to shove down my throat I've learned probably isn't real, even if it's true."

"Explain," Henry said in that focused, demanding way he had that usually irritated Jessie when it was geared at her. In this situation, she was grateful for it.

Quinn rolled her eyes. "You guys and your one-word commands," she muttered. Some of that languid relaxation in the chair tensed, and she didn't look quite so *at ease.* "I grew up in that compound, so at first you kind of have to take it all for truth. Like, oh, your mom didn't care about you, but she cared about the other one. The other one got everything and you got nothing. Don't you want revenge? Worked for a while."

"Then what?"

"Then she came to the compound," Quinn said, nodding her head toward Jessie. "I was thirteen. We were thirteen, I guess. And *I* had to go away. Couldn't have her knowing about me. Maybe the first couple years I resented it. All that *wilderness survival* training got a little old. But eventually, I got old enough and wise enough to the Peterson way of doing things. They brought me back and I realized I was just a tool. Tools don't matter. They're replaceable. So if I was—she was. But unlike her, I didn't have anywhere to go. That compound was all I'd ever had. So when I was supposed to slide into her place, I did."

Slide into her place. A cold bolt of unease trickled up Jessie's spine. She was always in her own place, so how could… "What do you mean?"

Quinn's dark eyes, the same deep brown as Jessie's own, locked with her. "Why do you think Rob didn't come after you for, like, ten years?"

Jessie froze—from the inside out. Like a ton of ice just encased her. "I hid," she managed to croak.

Quinn snorted. "No. *I* slid into place."

Jessie couldn't absorb it. Couldn't imagine… All those years of hiding and being careful so he'd never know Sarabeth existed and…Rob had thought she was still there, by his side?

"You're telling me she bailed, you *slid into place* and the guy didn't notice?" Henry returned, clearly not believing Quinn's story.

"Why would he notice? We're identical, mostly. He wanted her for her connection to the Petersons, for what she might know *or* what he might be able to use to get out of her—*our*—father. She was a tool. Someone replaces a tool with an identical copy, hard to notice."

"I can't believe this," Jessie said, shaking her head back and forth. "I can't." But the tool thing… Oh, she understood the tool thing.

Quinn shrugged, unbothered. "Guess you don't have to."

"Who wanted you to do it?"

Quinn flicked her gaze to Henry. There was a slight hesitation. "Daddy dearest."

"So why were you still doing his dirty work? Out here. Pointing a gun at Jessie."

"Didn't have a way out yet. I've got no ID. There's no record of me existing, far as I can tell. I have no money. No way to make it on my own. Oh, I was planning some things, but I hadn't gotten there yet. Then you came along, took the gun out of my hands and oops. I got caught. What better way to escape than that?"

"You aren't afraid of them?" Jessie asked, carefully. Quietly. "Tracking you down?"

Again, Quinn's dark gaze met her own and Jessie felt…a wave of sympathy for this woman. Maybe it was misplaced. Maybe this was all a lie. But something about all this…made it hard to think she wasn't telling the truth.

"I'm afraid of them when I'm on the inside, so what's the difference if I'm afraid of them on the outside? At least I have a chance out here. At least I call the shots out here." She glanced at Henry. "Or will."

Jessie understood that. All too well and to the letter. She slid a glance at Henry. He was frowning at Quinn, but it wasn't all disbelief. Maybe some disapproval. Definitely suspicion, but he was considering her words. Weighing them against what he knew.

But this wasn't all about Quinn, or even Jessie herself. "What do you think my daughter knows that she isn't telling me?"

Quinn's eyebrows rose. "She didn't tell you?"

"She was exhausted. Overwrought. I'm not going to press her."

"But you'll press your sister?"

"The grown adult sitting here that I barely know? Yes."

Quinn took some time to consider that, then with another one of her careless shrugs, settled back into her chair. "There was a little showdown between Rob and our father. Couple months back. I don't know what happened exactly, but when Rob came home he knew I wasn't you. He'd figured out he had a kid. He knew there were ways to use the kid."

"Use Sarabeth? He didn't care about Sarabeth."

"Care? No. Use? Yes. I mean, surely you know *you* don't matter to our dad, or you'd have been dead or back at the compound a decade ago. Wasn't any different for Rob and the kid. She was just a means to an end, a tool like you and me, but she was a new shiny one. And one he didn't think our father would pay much attention to. So he set out to get her."

It all made a terrible kind of sense. She'd thought it was about her. *Her* Peterson connection, but all Rob had done was tie her up in that basement. Been ready to kill her at the drop of a hat. But he'd let Sarabeth run. Explore.

Get caught up in stories of gold.

Jessie's stomach roiled so violently she was afraid she would be sick. She knew she needed to keep her cool. To work through this. But the idea Rob had been after Sarabeth… All this time she'd been so focused on herself. On *her* connections to the Petersons. Or Sarabeth's connection *through* her. She'd never considered it hadn't been about her at all.

She really was going to be sick. "I think I've heard enough." She got up and she bolted.

HENRY WANTED TO rush after Jessie, but he wasn't about to leave this woman alone. He believed Quinn, weirdly. But that didn't mean he trusted her.

"You're telling the truth," he said, hoping one of his brothers would return soon so he could check on Jessie.

Quinn shrugged. "Why wouldn't I be?"

"I'm sure there are as many reasons for that as there are for telling the truth." He studied her for another minute. "If you keep telling the truth, keep helping your *sister*, we'll help you, you know."

"Who's this mysterious *we*?"

"All of us here. If you're honest, and on the up and up, and don't put anyone here in danger, we'll do whatever it takes to keep you away from the people who want to hurt you."

"Sure you will, cowboy."

"It's a promise, Quinn. You don't have to believe it, but it's a promise nonetheless."

She said nothing to that, and Dunne returned. Henry was eager to go find Jessie, but then Landon grabbed him with information about the truck that had been driving past Jessie's apartment. By the time they were done poring over that material, the sun was rising and Henry didn't have a clue as to where Jessie was.

It bothered him, not because he figured she'd run off or done anything stupid, but because...

Because.

Frustrated with himself, he stalked through the house. Kate was up and making breakfast. When he passed Zara in the living room, she informed him Jessie was out in the stables, helping with some chores, but before he could go find her, he heard a clattering on the stairs.

Sarabeth bounded into the room, all bright eyes and energy. Her hair was tousled, but she was back in her clothes from yesterday—clearly, someone had washed them for her and given them back to her. She stopped when she saw him.

"Morning," she offered cheerfully. But she hesitated, like she didn't know what to do now that she'd seen him. Like she remembered this wasn't her house. Like she remembered they were in some kind of danger.

He didn't want her thinking about it. He wanted her having as much normal as possible, so he figured he'd have to act normal, too.

"Breakfast is on. Then you can earn your keep out in the stables."

Her eyes brightened. "Really? I can work with the horses?"

"Yeah, and it's work, so you better be ready."

She gave him a quick squeeze as she passed. "Thanks, Henry," she said, then she scurried into the kitchen.

Like she hadn't just killed him dead. They both did, mother and daughter, and it didn't matter what he told himself about it, all the excuses he tried to make. It wasn't about danger, about helping. It was about them.

Damn it.

Grumpy now, or even more so, he went to find Jessie in the stables. Jake was outside washing the truck— an unnecessary chore, which told Henry that everyone was making sure someone always had an eye on Jessie without making it too obvious.

Because it was the right thing to do. To help Jessie and Sarabeth as best they could—because they could.

Henry walked past Jake, trying not to think too hard about all these jangling emotions not shuffling into place—or away—like he could usually make them.

"I've got it from here," he said to Jake.

"I just bet you do." Jake grinned. "I'll finish all the same."

Henry grunted, his attitude not getting any better at Jake's cheerfulness. Still, he stepped into the stables. And all that irritation and anger just sort of leaked out. Because Jessie looked miserable. And beautiful, standing there stroking her hands down the horse's mane.

"Hey." Why did his voice sound so damn *affected*?

"Hi." She smiled or tried to. "Sorry I ditched you in there with Quinn." She sighed heavily. "I needed to get a handle on myself. I threw up." She closed her eyes and groaned. "I don't know why I told you that."

"I can handle a little puke."

It made her laugh, and it was…some kind of amazing he could make her do that. In the here and now. At all. When he was not exactly known for his humor.

"I just needed some…alone time to work it all out." She gestured helplessly at the horse.

"Yeah, I get that."

He looked at him with a wry smile. "I'm not sure you do until you have a child and are constantly surrounded."

"I have five brothers living on the same ranch. Isn't that the same thing?"

She laughed again and something in his chest expanded.

"Maybe." She sucked in a breath and let it out. She stood on nearly the opposite side of the stables. There was a strange kind of awkwardness in the silence that stretched out.

Even stranger, Henry didn't really know what to do about it.

Jessie cleared her throat and began to walk for the doors. "I should go check on Sarabeth."

"She's up. Eating breakfast." For a reason he could not explain to himself, he stopped her forward progress by stepping in her way. "We'll put her on light chore duty this morning, make her feel useful."

Jessie stopped walking, a good few yards in front of him, but she smiled. "She'll like that."

"What would you like?" he asked, taking a few steps forward.

Some of that bravado faded and her shoulders slumped. "For my daughter not to be at the center of all this. I can't stand the thought they're after *her*." Her voice broke, but she kept going. "That it isn't just protecting her from the fallout, but the actual...*thing*. About gold? But it's the reality. I have to figure out a way to deal with it." She looked up at him, and there were tears in her eyes. "And somehow thank you all for...doing all this when you didn't have to do."

It grated—not in an irritating way. Her thanks just scraped against him like... Like, he didn't know. "You don't have to thank me."

She nodded, but he could see she was going to lose the battle. The tears were going to win and though he grimaced a little, he also knew he couldn't just... stand there. He had to reach out. To pull her to him. He thought of what Sarabeth had told him back when he'd found her hiding out. Back rub. Say it's going to be okay. He could do that.

And Jessie didn't fight him on it. She leaned in. Relaxed. Cried. She smelled like horses and...her, and she seemed to fit right here, tucked up against him. She was so strong, held so much on her shoulders, but everyone needed a little...release sometimes.

He tended to choose things like lifting weights and chopping wood, but probably not the best suggestion. So he let her cry, and rubbed her back.

And he told her it was going to be okay, because he'd find a way to make sure it could be. Somehow.

She sniffled and began to pull away. "Well, you're not so bad at the comforting thing," she managed, wiping at her cheeks.

He had to fight the urge to wipe the tears himself, so

he chose to simply not let her go. "You can thank your daughter for that."

She looked up at him quizzically. His hands still on her shoulders.

"When I found her out there, she cried a bit. Then told me I did a terrible job with crying people and I should rub a back and say comforting things."

Jessie laughed through the tears. "That girl."

And she didn't step away, and he didn't let his hands fall. They just stood there in this weird world. Where he could comfort someone. Where he wanted to. Where he wanted to make everything right—familiar enough— but he didn't want to let go while he did it.

He didn't have a clue what was going on in her head, but she didn't back away. She held his gaze. And when he pulled her just a hair closer, when he tilted his head just so—

"Are you guys going to kiss?" Sarabeth's voice interrupted, making them both jump apart like guilty teenagers.

Sarabeth just stood there at the opening to the stables, looking at them both—not accusingly, but with a kind of innocent interest. "It looks like you are."

"Sarabeth," Jessie said firmly, but seemed at a loss as to what else to say.

"You can kiss him if you want, Mom."

Jessie closed her eyes. "Thank you for your permission," she muttered dryly. "But I think I'll go inside and get some breakfast."

And she moved—not a scurry exactly, but a very careful move that put a lot of distance between them—

out of the stables, leaving him with Sarabeth. Who studied him carefully.

"You should definitely kiss her," Sarabeth said after a while, nodding as if she'd come to the conclusion after thinking it over.

"You are something else, kid," he muttered.

"Why does everyone keep saying that?" she wondered aloud.

SARABETH DIDN'T SAY anything more about Henry kissing her mom while he showed her what to do with the horses, but she thought about it.

She wasn't dumb. She knew that if she got Henry to kiss Mom it wasn't like they'd magically get married and he'd be her dad and everything would be perfect. There was that lady who looked like Mom and someone shooting and the gold and all sorts of things that would complicate that.

But Sarabeth figured it didn't hurt to plan. *If* they did kiss, they might want to get married at *some* point. And if they *did* get married, Henry would be her stepdad, and maybe they could even live here with the horses.

And Henry would always protect them, and Mom wouldn't have to worry so much. And Sarabeth could keep Henrietta the cat and get a dog and...

Well, she couldn't get too excited about that yet. First, she had to work out a plan. Step by step. And the first step was Mom and Henry kissing.

Henry gave her a little carrot to feed the horse and she squealed in delight when the horse ate it. "Horses are so cool."

"Well, as long as you're staying here, you'll be helping with them. It's called earning your keep."

"What does my mom have to do to earn her keep?"

Henry made a strangled kind of noise, though Sarabeth couldn't figure out why. "Whatever needs doing, I suppose," he finally said. "Lots of people equal lots of chores."

"I like the lots of people. *And* horses," Sarabeth said. "And cats and dogs and ranches." She looked up at him through her lashes. "And you."

"Thought I was mean," he said in that rumbly voice Sarabeth was beginning to recognize as discomfort.

"You can be. I like that, too. I'm mean sometimes. Mom says it's okay, as long as it's geared toward the right people, and if you end up being mean and wrong you apologize."

"Guess she's right."

"She's right a lot," Sarabeth replied. Then wondered if that was something Henry would like. Maybe *he* liked being right a lot? She frowned a little and rubbed the horse while Henry moved to a different stable.

He came back with two shovels, one big, one a little smaller. He handed her the smaller one. "Poop duty."

Sarabeth wrinkled her nose. "Gross."

"Yeah, it is. Lots of things that are cool come with gross parts. You gotta be willing to handle the hard, gross stuff if you want the good parts."

Sarabeth wasn't sure she agreed with that, but she let Henry teach her how to shovel up the poop and put it in the bucket. It was smelly, but she tried to think of it like she was helping out Sammy the horse.

"You know, it's a good life lesson," Henry said after a while. "Gross parts and good parts are a part of life."

"Okay."

Henry sighed, then he took the shovel from her when they were done. He put his hand on her shoulder.

She liked when he did that. It was like when Mom ran her hand over her hair. It felt…like care.

Then he crouched and got eye to eye with her. He looked serious and Sarabeth's heartbeat got a little fast in her chest.

"You're going to have to tell your mom the whole truth. All of it."

Panic started to creep in. "What do you mean?"

"I mean whatever it is. You've been keeping stuff hidden. I know you don't want to get in trouble, but…" He trailed off, his eyebrows scrunching together, and he studied her hard enough she wanted to run away. Hide. "You're not afraid of getting in trouble. You're trying to protect her." He seemed…surprised by that.

Sarabeth tried to use that surprise and bolt, but Henry held her firm. Not hard like her father had, but *firm*. Gentle. But she still couldn't wriggle away.

"Running's not solving this problem, Sarabeth. Face it. You've got guts, kid. Use them."

Guts. She liked to think she was brave. Strong. *Guts*. But she didn't want Mom to be worried. She didn't want Mom to know… But Henry… He knew. He didn't *know* know, but he kind of knew. And she wanted him to protect them, didn't she? Wasn't that why she came to him in the first place?

His other hand rested on her shoulder, and his eyes

were… Well, they were more like Mom's. He was waiting for her answer, not shouting. He wanted something from her, but not just that and then he'd turn around and disappear.

"Sarabeth."

"I don't want her to be scared. I don't want her to cry." And she didn't want to cry herself.

"I get that. And I can't promise she won't be scared. I can't promise she won't cry, but, Sarabeth, if you tell us all the truth—all of us—we can figure out how you *and* your mom don't have to be scared anymore. You came to me because you thought I could handle this, right?"

She nodded, not trusting herself to speak.

"Then I need you to let me handle it by telling me everything, but your mom has to be there, okay? She has to know, too."

Chapter Fourteen

Jessie felt more herself after she ate something, and then helped Kate with the breakfast dishes. She still felt... on edge, but more equipped to handle it.

She wasn't going to dwell on what had happened in the stables—not the *moment*, and certainly not her daughter suggesting she could kiss Henry.

Kiss him! Ha! What a disaster that would be.

Probably an enjoyable disaster, but still a disaster. She wasn't a young, dumb teenager trying to escape any longer. She wasn't going to let a man sweep in and save her and kiss her and...

Jessie squeezed her eyes shut for a moment as she washed down the kitchen table. Henry wasn't Rob, and it wasn't fair to compare them. She wasn't even the same Jessie she'd been all those years ago.

But she was not kissing Henry. Certainly not before this whole daughter-in-danger, identical twin, gold thing was sorted.

After...

Well, there was no point even considering *after* now when they were still so in the dark.

She heard the front door squeak open, the low sounds of conversation, and then Sarabeth trudged into the kitchen. She no longer looked excited about horses or kissing. She looked…upset.

Jessie left the washcloth on the table and crossed to her. "What's wrong, baby?"

Before Sarabeth could answer, Henry entered. Sarabeth looked up at him, and Jessie almost jumped to accuse him of upsetting her daughter, but his expression stopped her.

Underneath that careful veneer of stoic military man, there was this tightness around his mouth. Worry.

"Sarabeth, I'm going to give you the choice, okay?" Henry began. "You can tell your mom everything just the two of you. But she's going to need to fill me in. Or you can tell both of us. But I'm going to have to tell everyone what's going on. So the last alternative is telling everyone yourself. It's up to you what you want to do."

Jessie didn't have a clue as to what was going on, but she pulled Sarabeth close. "You don't have to do anything in front of anyone, sweetheart. Let's—"

"I want to tell everyone."

"Sarabe—"

"Mom. It's the right thing to do." She sounded so adult. So sure. It was like getting a flash of the woman she'd become someday. Jessie didn't know how to argue with it. "I don't really have answers, just stuff Rob told me. Stuff I heard Rob say. I knew it would upset you, so let's tell everyone. Everyone here wants to help."

Jessie looked up at Henry. She wanted to…blame him, somehow, for how much Sarabeth was taking on her shoulders. But that was hardly Henry's fault. Henry hadn't put them in this situation. In fact, he'd been dragged into it by the both of them.

"Can I go get Henrietta first?" Sarabeth asked, looking up at Henry.

"Uh, where *is* Henrietta?"

Sarabeth's expression went sheepish. "Wellll…"

"In my room wreaking havoc, no doubt. All right, go get her. Maybe clean up the worst of it? We'll get everyone together in the living room in about fifteen."

Sarabeth nodded, but before she scurried off she looked at Jessie. Her expression went firm. Determined. "It's going to be okay, Mom." Then she dashed off, no doubt excited about cat wrangling.

Jessie slowly stood, trying to get her bearings. Trying to figure out the right thing to say.

But Henry spoke first. "We'll gather everyone up in the living room. She can say her piece. No one will pressure her. I promise you that, and if she needs to stop to take a break, just take her upstairs."

Jessie nodded. It was strange. All these years of being a single mom, she'd never really believed anyone else had Sarabeth's best interests at heart. She'd never let anyone close enough for that to happen.

But she believed in the Thompson brothers. Henry in particular. She just wished she could wash away the heavy cloud of guilt. "It kills me to know she's been keeping something from me. That she's standing there measuring *me* when it should be the other way around.

"You've done plenty of reassuring and it shows. She's a tough kid. And she loves you. She wants to protect you."

"It's not supposed to be that way, though."

"I think it is. I think that's the way love is always supposed to be."

It felt very strange to be discussing love, but she knew he was talking about mothers and children. Not *love*.

"Maybe we should take this private moment to discuss what happened in the stables."

Jessie was surprised. Shocked, actually, that he'd bring it up, not let it go. She cleared her throat. "Ah, what would that be?"

"Sarabeth suggesting I kiss you."

"Oh, that. Well." She was otherwise speechless. What was she supposed to say? *You're welcome to?* Because she was…too curious, but also this was so not the time and…

"I just want to make it clear, if I ever do kiss you, it won't be because your daughter brought it up. It'll be because I think about you too damn much."

Jessie opened her mouth, but no words came out. Maybe because every coherent thought just…melted out of her.

I think about you too damn much.

Wow.

Luckily, she didn't have to think of anything to say. Jake came in through the kitchen door, already talking. "Zara won't be long. Hazeleigh's at the fort, but Landon thought he could fill her in later. Not sure about Cal."

Dunne and Quinn appeared from the door to his quarters. "Cal's coming. Finishing up some research." Dunne frowned at Quinn behind him. "Should she really be a part of this?" Dunne asked.

"Should *you*?" Quinn returned, looking pointedly at his bad leg.

"Living room," Henry ordered. "Everyone," he said. A clear response to Dunne's initial question.

Jessie wondered as well if Quinn should be part of it, but... Well, Quinn was *part* of this. Maybe they couldn't trust her yet, but maybe it would turn out she had information they needed. Maybe it would turn out she actually had...a sister.

She watched Quinn follow Dunne out, then Jake. Everyone talked. Joked. Touched. And when she reached Henry, he put his hand on the small of her back. Like he was somehow...hers.

She looked up at him, and his gaze lowered to hers.

"Too damn much," he muttered, looking back ahead, where his family had arranged themselves to deal with *her* problem. What Sarabeth knew. What danger they were all in.

And it didn't matter who was the reason, she realized. No one blamed anyone. They saw a problem, and they came together to fix it.

Jessie found...that was the kind of group she wanted to be a part of. Wanted her daughter to learn from. Not guilt. Not worry.

Teamwork.

THE FAMILY HAD GATHERED. Henry studied them all. Sarabeth playing with the kitten, curled up next to Jessie in the oversize chair. Hazeleigh and Zara sandwiching Jake on the couch, while Landon sat on the arm next to Hazeleigh, who'd come back from the fort. Cal had dragged in chairs from the kitchen table, and he, Quinn and Dunne had settled into those. Kate sat crosslegged on the floor, Brody standing next to her, leaning against the wall.

Henry stood in front of them all. He'd called the "meeting" so to speak, so it was up to him to move it along. But there was something about the moment—they weren't a biological family, but something about the ways they'd all come together had created…this. Maybe Jessie, Sarabeth and Quinn weren't a part of it, but they seemed to slot right in.

Every part had its function, and now they needed to work together to solve the problem.

But the eleven-year-old girl snuggling the cat within an inch of its life was going to have to explain the problem to them first.

"We're all mostly up to speed on what's been going down the last few days, and even some of the backstory for everybody, but Sarabeth has some information that might help us make sure everyone's safe," Henry began. "That's the goal here. Everyone can go about their normal lives without worrying about any threats."

"No one's interested in the gold?" Quinn asked, studying her nails with fake disinterest. Henry could tell she read the room very carefully, and Henry couldn't decide if that was a comfort or suspicious.

Dunne muttered darkly. Landon and Hazeleigh gave an emphatic *no* simultaneously. The only one who seemed the least bit interested in gold was Sarabeth herself.

As Jessie had said in the stables: *that girl.*

Henry gave her a disapproving look, and she wrinkled her nose in return.

"This gold seems to be the cause of a lot of problems, and an answer to absolutely none. Men have been murdered. Lives have been threatened. But it's bigger than that, isn't it, Sarabeth?"

"Sort of," Sarabeth agreed. She sat there with the kitten, then decided to come stand by Henry. She faced down all the adults in the room. She didn't crumple with everyone's eyes on her. Much like that night when she'd faced down the police, she held herself very still. And she focused on her mother.

Henry knew that was where she got her strength.

"There's supposed to be a whole house," Sarabeth said.

"A house?" Jessie replied, clearly hearing this for the first time.

"Full of stuff. Gold and money and some kind of jewelry thing. Some guy was a robber, back a long time ago, and he kept all this stuff in one house. Hidden away. And the story is his kids thought it was cursed or something, so when he died they just left it there."

Henry could feel Cal's gaze cut to him, and Cal didn't need to say anything for Henry to know what he was thinking.

You can't be serious.

"But some people had clues, I guess, and joined clubs to find it or something. And some of the groups tried to make it look like it didn't exist so no one would look for it, and some of the groups fought and hurt each other until there was basically only one left."

"Led by my father," Jessie said, sounding shaken, but certain.

Sarabeth shrugged. "Rob complained a lot about *them*, but he didn't say anyone specifically. Just said they were dumb or angry, but he was smart. There's clues somewhere, I guess, but they've never been able to find where. Rob was looking for a map. That's why he killed the museum guy. He thought he had it. He didn't, but he had pictures that led them to some of the gold, but not the house with the other stuff."

"You sure know a lot, kid," Quinn said. Her gaze was sharp on Sarabeth, and it wasn't kind, but considering.

Henry angled his body to put a buffer between Quinn and Sarabeth.

"So a bunch of men are after a house full of—" Henry searched for a word that wasn't *treasure*, because he was pretty sure that would send Cal off the deep end "—valuable stuff."

Sarabeth nodded. "They have a bunch of plans when they get the money. Like bombs and stuff. I didn't understand it exactly, but they don't like the government."

"Now *that* makes some sense," Cal replied. "A group of antigovernment militia types, living in a compound, dreaming up fake riches."

"But they aren't fake," Sarabeth said. "The gold was real."

Cal didn't say anything to that.

"The gold was real," Henry agreed to keep Sarabeth from getting insulted enough to stop talking. "And it doesn't matter if the rest is real. If they *think* it is, that's all that matters. They'll keep looking for it."

"Because it's *real*," Sarabeth insisted. "It has to be."

Henry knew Cal wanted to argue with her, and he watched the way Quinn very carefully watched her. He didn't like that. Not at all. So he mentioned something about feeding the other kittens and convinced Kate to take Sarabeth out to do just that.

And keep her out of earshot.

"So we've got a houseful of treasure somewhere," Cal said, sounding derisive.

But Jessie was chewing on her bottom lip, that clear sign she was worrying over something. "A map," she said, her eyebrows drawing together. "Sarabeth said he was looking for a map."

"What, like you know where it is?" Quinn demanded.

"I'm not sure."

Henry was gratified that Jessie studied Quinn with a careful kind of suspicion. Quinn seemed to realize her enthusiasm *was* suspicious.

"What do you know about the map?" Henry asked Quinn.

Quinn scowled, crossing her arms over her chest. "That they think it exists, and is the great, majestic answer to all their problems. The kid's right. Mostly. Antigovernment. Militia. That sort of thing keeps them focused, but at the end of the day, it's the treasure hunt. They want to find it—they can claim these grand plans once they do, but they're obsessed with the hunt. And beating each other to it."

"Each other? There's more than Rob going against our father?"

Quinn's gaze on Jessie was cool. Henry knew he

could be reading into things, but he saw a kind of… resentment in the identical dark eyes. "Every now and again. Different factions of the same messed up whatever. Work together when it's them against the world, but it happens that they sometimes want the whole piece of the pie and go off alone."

"I don't follow," Dunne muttered.

"*You* wouldn't," Quinn returned.

"That the whole truth, Quinn?" Henry asked.

She turned that cool gaze on him. And kept it there. He'd give her points for that. "Nothing is the whole truth when it comes to the Petersons."

"I'm not talking about the Petersons. I'm talking about you."

She flicked a gaze to Jessie, but then turned it back to him. She seemed to consider things. "We've got George in one camp. We've got Gene in the other."

Jessie frowned. "Who's Gene?"

"Our father's brother. Less group, more recluse, but he's always one step ahead of George, and George hates it. But neither of them have found the jackpot. Both are on the hunt for the map. Rob thought it was here. George was following some cockamamie old story about it being in Oregon. Gene… Well, no one quite knows what Gene thinks, no matter how George tries to smoke him out."

"This sounds like a bunch of family insanity to me," Cal said. "*Your* family insanity. Not mine."

"Then feel free to butt out," Quinn replied, faking a sweet smile.

"People are in danger," Henry said, keeping his tone

cool and calm rather than reactionary. "We'll help them get out of danger, no matter whose family is involved."

Cal sent him a sharp, disapproving look, but said nothing.

"So what's the next step?" Dunne asked.

"I think we need to find out who's casing Jessie's house." He nodded at Landon.

Landon stood to address the group. "We did some digging on the truck Hazeleigh saw driving by the apartment the day Sarabeth ran away. The license is stolen, the truck isn't registered anywhere I can find, and with the blacked-out windows we couldn't get an idea of who was driving. There's still a few more avenues I want to prod, but the bottom line is I think we can be assured this isn't a coincidence. That truck is looking for Jessie. Or Sarabeth."

"We want to find out who's driving. And why," Henry reiterated. "I think we should go into town. You have a stagecoach shift this afternoon, right, Jessie?"

"Yes," she replied. She looked like she wanted to say something else, but bit her lip instead.

Henry would prod on that later.

"Good. I'll go with Jessie on that. We'll look out for followers. And to make things interesting, we'll bring in the twin."

"Huh?" Quinn replied.

"One of you will go with Quinn to Jessie's apartment," Henry said to his brothers. "We'll see where we get a follow. And if we can circle around and get something out of them."

"Why should I agree to that?" Quinn demanded.

"Why shouldn't you?" Dunne returned.

Quinn scowled at him. "Fine. Whatever. Just not with these two dour Dans." She pointed at Landon. "You look fun."

Hazeleigh frowned a little, but that wasn't why Henry wanted a different option. "Landon's on computer duty with whatever we might find. Sorry, you're going to have to pick one of the dour Dans."

"Ugh," Quinn said, but she didn't argue.

Chapter Fifteen

The morning went by in a blur. Jessie kept trying to get Henry alone, but it was a no-go with so many people around, making arrangements. The men seemed to talk in a military code that wasn't so much incomprehensible as confusing.

Sarabeth clung close. Even knowing she'd be well watched over, Jessie wasn't looking forward to leaving her behind when she went into town. But it had to be done.

Especially with what Jessie had to tell Henry.

She just needed him alone. She couldn't say what needed to be said in front of Quinn. Not until she knew for sure Quinn would protect Sarabeth above herself.

Jessie changed back into her own clothes, since someone had been kind enough to wash hers and put them in Henry's room. Sarabeth sat cross-legged in the middle of the bed with Henrietta—and Jessie knew that once all this danger was over, Sarabeth would be begging to take the kitten home with them.

"Are you and Henry going to be alone?" Sarabeth asked, looking down at the cat who purred in her lap.

Jessie thought about the stables, this morning, Sarabeth asking if they were going to kiss. Embarrassment and something else shifted through her, but she tried to push it away. "Sarabeth..."

"It's just, I didn't say something I maybe should have. Henry wanted me to be honest, and I was. Mostly. But..."

Embarrassment forgotten, Jessie turned to stare at her daughter, worry and panic sprouting anew. "But what?"

"The real thing I didn't tell you wasn't the house. I mean, I didn't tell you that because I knew you wouldn't really believe it."

Jessie opened her mouth to argue, but then shut it. She wouldn't have. She barely believed in this gold and she'd seen it with her own eyes.

"Okay, so what's the real thing?" Jessie asked, trying to remain calm. Trying to find her equilibrium in this constant whirl of change and confusion.

"I didn't want to say in front of Quinn. I kind of like her, and lots of what she said is the truth as I know it." Sarabeth frowned deeper. "But I don't know if she'd keep me safe, like I know everyone else would."

Jessie couldn't fault her for that. Jessie had the same kinds of concerns. "Okay, what else?"

"Rob talked to somebody on the phone. A lot. Somebody who told him what to do. I don't know who it was, but Rob told him about me. I think that might be who's looking at the apartment."

Jessie had to stand very still and work very hard to breathe normally. This wasn't new information per se.

This was just…more of Sarabeth being the target. It gave more context. It wasn't new.

And they were handling it. But still… "Sarabeth, why would you run away knowing someone might be after you?"

"So he'd stay away from you." Her voice pitched and she sat up on her knees. "So you'd know Henry had to help!" She slumped back down, chin to chest. "So maybe I could find the stuff and then nobody could hurt anybody," she muttered.

Jessie sighed. "And this is it? All you know?"

Sarabeth looked up, her eyes a little shiny, but Jessie knew she wasn't going to cry. "Yes. I promise. I *promise*."

Jessie swallowed down all the fear and worry. She wanted Sarabeth to look at her and see certainty. Know she'd be protected and everything would be okay.

It had to be okay. For her daughter. "All right. Henry and I will discuss that." Plus what Jessie had to tell him. "We'll get to the bottom of this, and we'll make sure everyone's safe."

"Even Quinn?"

Torn, Jessie sat down on the corner of the bed. She took Sarabeth's hand in hers and met her daughter's worried gaze. "I don't know. There's still a lot we don't know about Quinn."

Before she could say more, Henry appeared at the doorway. "Ready?"

Jessie managed a thin smile and a nod. No, she wasn't ready, but a lot had to be dealt with. "Now, Sarabeth, while we're gone you need to be on your best behavior."

Sarabeth nodded, studying them both.

"Jake and Zara have some horse chores for you, if you're up to it," Henry offered.

Sarabeth nodded emphatically, but she held Henrietta to her chest. "Can she come with?"

Henry eyed the kitten. "Best to keep her out of the way of the horses. Maybe let her play with her brothers and sisters for a bit."

Sarabeth considered, then sighed. "Okay, I guess."

They went downstairs together, and Jessie wasn't sure why that felt…odd. Maybe because it felt cozy. Like a normal… Well, not family, since they weren't one, but unit? Something.

They met Cal and Quinn at the bottom of the stairs. Jake and Zara were there too, all ready to sweep Sarabeth away to do something. Keep her mind occupied. Keep her safe.

Jessie didn't know how she'd gotten so lucky to have all…*this*. Sure, none of the gold, Peterson, daughter-in-danger stuff was lucky, but it had almost always been her life. Help and protection had *never* been a part of it.

She said her goodbyes to Sarabeth, warning her once more to be on her best behavior. Then she followed Henry, Cal and Quinn outside. Cal and Quinn got into a truck, and Jessie followed Henry to his.

"The chores, the animals, giving her something to do so she feels productive. You're good with her. I didn't see that one coming," Jessie said.

"She's not so bad."

Jessie didn't have the slightest clue why that charmed

her. Something about the gruff, uncomfortable way he said it.

They got in the car and she hadn't even clicked on her seat belt when he asked her a question that surprised her. "Did she tell you whatever else?"

"How did you know there was whatever else?"

"I saw the way she looked at Quinn, then stuck close to you. She had something else on her mind, but she didn't want to say it in front of the question mark."

"Perceptive. Someone knows about Sarabeth."

"I figured."

"She heard Rob talk to someone. She made it sound like someone was telling Rob what to do. I always figured him for the ringleader, but it seems not."

"Makes sense. He had a fake wife for ten years. He definitely wasn't fully in charge."

Jessie shuddered at the thought. "I don't trust her. I can't. But I feel for her."

"Yeah, well, I don't trust her, either."

"And you don't feel for her?"

Henry flicked a glance at her. "I feel for people I care about. So no. Not at the moment."

Jessie knew she shouldn't wonder if she was one of those people he cared about. If Sarabeth was. It didn't matter. Whether he felt for them or not, he'd protect them. And that was all that mattered.

"Landon will be at the computer," he explained. "Anything we see, or Cal and Quinn see, we text to him and he'll do his thing. Mostly, we're just feeling out who's looking for you and Sarabeth. No action. Just information gathering. So all you have to do is drive the stagecoach thing and keep your eyes peeled."

"Okay, but… Henry, there's something else."

He muttered what sounded like a curse under his breath. "Is there ever not going to be?"

"This is a new something else. Something Sarabeth and Quinn said that made me remember. I hadn't thought much about it—I'd been so concerned about Sarabeth and what she'd done to Rob and all that, but when they said *map*, I remembered." Jessie inhaled. She'd considered keeping this to herself. Handling it herself, but maybe she'd learned that wouldn't do.

Maybe Henry had no reason to help her, but he wanted to. Or needed to. Or something. And God knew she needed help. "There was just this…odd map. In my grandmother's belongings that I got after she died." Jessie swallowed. "I never knew what it was. But I…" She looked at Henry's harsh profile. "Henry, Sarabeth mentioned a map, and obviously I don't have a clue if it's *the* map, but… I didn't take it with me after Grandma died. I just knew… I knew if I was going to my father's family, I didn't want to bring her things. I didn't want… I just knew it wouldn't be mine."

"So what did you do with it?"

"It's kind of weird."

Henry laughed, and she'd always considered that laugh bitter, but maybe it wasn't so much bitter as fatalistic.

"What about this isn't weird?" he returned.

Fair enough. "So my grandmother used to visit my grandfather's grave every week. And her parents'. She brought them flowers, tidied up, that kind of thing, and she showed me how her father had this thing in his stone. It was put in there to hide alcohol during prohibition. You unscrew this part and people would hide booze in there, but obviously it wasn't used anymore so I… I put the stuff in there. A necklace, her rings and the papers I didn't understand."

"This map, that they've been looking for for decades, is hidden in a gravestone."

"I don't know for sure. My grandmother wasn't a Peterson. She shouldn't be connected to this. It was a map that made no sense to me at thirteen. Maybe it's nothing."

"And maybe it's everything."

HENRY HAD TO figure out how to proceed. He had no interest in finding some treasure—whether it was real or fake—but maybe finding it ended the nonsense surrounding it.

He doubted it, but it was a step anyway. For the time being, Jessie had work to do. They had a stalker of some kind to suss out. All before they could go find a *map* hidden in a *gravestone*.

And he'd thought being in a secret military group to take down terrorist organizations had been complicated.

"If it's a map that leads us to this…house of treasure or whatever we want to call it, that groups of people have been after for decades far as I can tell, what do we do?" she asked, staring out the window.

That *was* the question. "I think we need to make sure it's there first. And that no one's following us when we do." But how to make that happen. Whoever was after Sarabeth knew Jessie had a twin, likely had an inkling said twin had been "taken" by those helping Jessie.

He drove into town, keeping his eye on anything that might appear out of the ordinary. He drove past where Cal and Quinn had parked in front of the hardware store.

Henry didn't slow. He trusted Cal to handle whoever might be after Quinn. His job was to keep Jessie safe. So he drove her out to the stagecoach main offices and stables, between Wilde and Bent.

When he parked, Jessie hesitated. "They want Sarabeth. They think she knows something. And I'm going to go to work?"

"Just remember, we've got seven people at that ranch keeping an eye on her. Out of everyone, she's the safest."

"But if they think she knows and Quinn and I don't—" She looked up at him, desperate for some assurances.

"I think Quinn knows quite a bit, and they know it. They'd assume Sarabeth told you anything. They might want her, but that doesn't make you disposable. I think that means any one of you could be a target."

Jessie sighed. "I don't know how this got so out of hand."

"Probably around the time someone decided, 'I know, I'm going to dedicate my life to finding some 1800s bank robber's cache.'"

Jessie managed a smile at that. She got out of the truck, but stopped when he started to do the same. "Stay here. I have to check in and talk to the manager and a few other things. They'll think it's strange if you're hulking around me the whole time."

"I don't hulk, and you aren't going anywhere alone."

"Maybe *hulk* was the wrong word, but it's weird to have someone following me around, particularly a large, intimidating man. So actually, hulking was apt. It arouses suspicion, doesn't it? You following me *everywhere*. And shouldn't we avoid that?"

Henry scowled. He didn't want her going anywhere on her own.

"Unless they're lying in wait here, at the stagecoach company, you'll be able to see if anyone suspicious comes in. You can step in then. But for the time being, I need to be able to do this normally. Not just for looks, but for myself. I can handle some things myself. I *have* to be able to call some of the shots myself. In order to come out on the other side of this, I need that, okay? I don't need a protector."

Henry couldn't look at her, so he stared straight ahead. He understood what she was saying. He even agreed with her. The problem wasn't her or that, it was this…thing inside him. This desperate need.

And it wasn't about the way he'd failed his mother—at least not fully. Though he knew that was what Jessie thought. Maybe he should let her think that. But…

"No, you probably don't need one, but I need you to let me protect you and Sarabeth anyway."

"I've tried to tell you I don't want to be some stand-in for the things you think you did wrong."

"Not that," Henry muttered. "Not all."

"Then what?"

It was a wonder the steering wheel didn't bend under the strength of his grip. He kept staring straight ahead, still seated in the driver's seat. If he didn't hold on to the wheel, he might grab on to her.

And something about that made the truth seem... necessary. He was a man who prided himself on facing the realities of the situation, and whether or not he liked it, the reality was simple. "I care about the both of you."

There was a sharp inhale at that, but he wasn't about to look over and see what kind of expression was on her face. It was a fact. Didn't mean he had to deal with the aftermath of the facts. "Aren't you going to be late?"

"Are you going to stay here?"

"Yeah. Unless I see something."

"Good." She began to walk toward the building, and he stayed in the driver's seat. But he watched her. She took four steps and then stopped, turned. Met his gaze as she walked back to the truck.

"Something about the way you say you care about us like it's the worst possible thing just... I don't know." She fisted a hand at her heart. "Makes it mean more."

He frowned at her. "That's messed up."

She laughed. "Probably."

But he supposed that was the thing. What would he do with not messed up? He wouldn't have a clue.

"I think we're both a little messed up," she continued, and her gaze was earnest. Studying. He didn't know why they were having this conversation here. Now.

"Guess most people are," he returned, rather than stopping it. Telling her to go inside. Telling her to get back in the truck so he could tuck her away and handle it himself. Alone. Like he should.

But he didn't. Because she needed to be part of it. She needed to stand on her own two feet, and he understood that better than anything else.

No one could fight your demons for you.

"I guess so." But before she turned and left, she leaned in and brushed her lips across his cheek. "Thank you," she said.

He was too puzzled—by the chaste kiss and the genuine thanks—to simply let it go. "For what?"

"Protecting. Caring." She smiled a little and backed away from the car. "Being good with Sarabeth when so many people, men especially, have hurt her. She needs that. I need that for her. I'll be right back."

She turned and strode for the office building. Henry watched her go. He didn't know what to make of any of that, and there wasn't yet time to figure it out. He supposed there would be.

He'd make sure there would be. Which meant getting to the end of this mystery and danger.

Chapter Sixteen

Jessie wasn't as on edge as she had been. It was likely stupidity on her part, but the idea Henry *needed* to act as some kind of protector, because he cared about both her and Sarabeth, had settled…something.

Aside from all that emotional stuff, there was the fact it was hard to feel like a target when a large, former military man sat next to you, scanning the world around you with a steely-eyed concentration she trusted meant he saw anything and everything.

He cared. *Cared.* And she wasn't foolish enough to think that it didn't have anything to do with his past failures at protecting people, which probably weren't even failures. Just felt like them. But she also knew a man like Henry didn't grumpily admit care if it wasn't there.

And she felt the same. She was scared of it. Unsure about what it meant for the future. It complicated…so many things.

But it was there.

Before they could deal with that, though, they had to figure out a way to make sure Sarabeth was safe.

She smiled at those who handed their tickets to

Henry. Answered questions. Led the horses around the stagecoach trail. She could almost pretend this was just a normal day.

Almost.

She dropped the last ticket holders off at their requested stop closer to Wilde than Bent. She still had about an hour left on her shift, and she'd just ride the circuit unless she got word that more tickets had been bought.

"Stop," Henry said, one of those gruff orders that had her obeying before she fully thought it through.

She frowned at him. They were basically in the middle of nowhere, between two of the stagecoach stops, between the two main towns. "What?"

"That the cemetery your grandfather is buried at?" he asked, pointing at the hill. Gravestones dotted the roll of green grass. This was the back side and her grandfather was buried at the front side that faced Wilde— you could see almost the entire town from the top of that hill.

"Yes."

"We've taken all the tickets, right? Dropped everyone off. Why not go look now? We'll just do it really quick before your shift is up."

"It's off the path."

Henry gave her a *seriously?* kind of look.

"I'm not supposed to take the coach off the path." She watched impatience pass over his face before he schooled it away.

"All right."

That was just another thing about him. He could be

bossy and pushy, but it was about the right things. He picked his battles. Carefully.

"Although, sometimes we're allowed to go off path if it's a particular customer request." She gave him a sheepish smile. "And they pay."

"Fine. Consider it a request and I'll pony up at the office after."

"I'll pay you back once I—"

"No, you won't. Come on now. Before your shift is over."

She frowned at his steamroll. She'd pay him back. One way or another. But for now she turned the horses. There was an old, overgrown path here into the back of the cemetery. She let the horses up as far as she could before the path got too narrow for the coach. She could tie the horses to the bench there, and they'd be able to keep horses and coach in view as they walked over to the other side of the hill.

Henry got down, and she gripped the reins and followed suit. But Henry was there by the time her feet hit the ground.

He took the reins from her and secured them to the bench. "We won't go too far. We'll get a lay of the land, and if it looks safe, we'll get the map. If not, we'll come back."

Jessie nodded. He paused for a second, then took her hand in his. Sort of like the other night when they'd been out looking for Sarabeth. But this was more... casual. Friendly.

Care.

They began to walk up the hill. The cemetery was

mostly older gravestones, some tilted or sinking with age. Some even broken so that large grass grew around the pieces as the mower likely couldn't get close enough easily.

The breeze was cool, the sun was warm and Henry's hand was firm and rough. She looked up at him, almost haloed by all that golden sun. He didn't have pretty words. He didn't offer promises of some grand future together. Rob had done both those things.

Henry simply offered his gruff protection. Because it was the right thing to do, and what had shaped him as a child meant he felt compelled to follow right. Because her daughter had climbed under all those angry defenses to the softhearted man underneath.

But why did he care about *her* when she'd done nothing but cause him trouble?

Her thoughts came to an abrupt halt and she stopped when she heard voices. Henry stopped, too. She shaded her eyes against the sun. As they reached the top she saw a little group of people. They appeared to be doing something…maybe cleaning the graves?

"Should we just turn back?" she said to Henry, even as a few heads turned toward them.

"Don't want to be suspicious. We'll come back and do what we need to later," Henry said. "For now we'll keep going and you can pretend to give me some kind of historical lecture."

"I don't know any historical lectures."

"Just try to think of stuff your grandmother told you. Think quick, though. Here comes Mrs. Caruthers."

Mrs. Caruthers. Jessie frowned at that. Why would she be out here when she should be at her store?

"Well, hello, Jessie. Now, where have you and your girl disappeared to? And who's this?" She narrowed her eyes at Henry. "One of those Thompson brothers, aren't you?"

Henry smiled, and it was dangerously close to being a *charming* smile. Who knew he could fake charm?

"Yes, ma'am."

"Well, that's interesting. What are two young people doing holding hands walking through the cemetery? Unless you were hoping to find some alone time."

"Jessie was just offering me some historical background of the town."

Mrs. Caruthers smiled at that and beamed at Jessie. "Your grandmother would be proud. Nothing more important than history. Family. Connection." She nodded emphatically then turned her attention back to Henry. "You watch after this one. Her grandmother was a dear, dear friend of mine."

Which wasn't true. Grandma hadn't cared much for Mrs. Caruthers at all. She'd called her a harmless gossip, when she was being generous. But Jessie could see why Mrs. Caruthers might not remember it that way—Mrs. Caruthers often thought people liked her because she had gossip to spread. Not that they just tolerated her *for* the gossip.

"What is all this?" Henry asked, still with that pleasant, nonthreatening smile. It was almost like he made himself seem smaller. Not at all lethal, when Jessie knew he most certainly was.

"Oh, I'm part of the Wilde Historical Society. Hazeleigh suggested we do some work cleaning up the cemetery a few months back. She saw something online about that sort of thing." Mrs. Caruthers rolled her eyes. "We finally got around to doing it. You've got some people buried here, don't you, Jessie?"

"Uh, yes. Yes, I do." Grandma. The grandfather she'd never known. Great-grandparents and likely Petersons as far back as the gravestones went. She'd never thought of it as *having people*.

Maybe she should have, but she'd always felt so disconnected from "family" unless it was her grandmother.

"Why don't you point them out? We'll clean them up for you."

Jessie tried to fix on a smile. "Oh, no. Just follow whatever plan you had. I'm not one for cemeteries, really. I haven't even visited my grandmother's grave since I've been back."

"A shame," Mrs. Caruthers said, sounding disapproving. "But then, why are you here?"

"Ah, my fault. Jessie mentioned history and this place and I drug her along."

"I thought you lived with two historian types. But you chose Jessie?"

Henry smiled again, then leaned forward in an almost conspiratorial manner. "Well, I may have had ulterior motives."

Mrs. Caruthers laughed and patted Henry's arm. She

left her hand there and blushed a little. "My, ranch work does wonders for a body, doesn't it? Never did for my Al, but…" She patted his arm a few more times. Then laughed a little breathlessly. "Well, anyway. I won't keep you any longer. You two have your walk or what have you." She winked and then made her way back to her group.

"We'll walk around a bit more then head back," Henry said, his voice quiet.

"Let's avoid my great-grandparents' graves. I don't want her getting it into her head to clean them."

Henry nodded and they walked the perimeter of the cemetery as much as they could while also keeping the horses in view.

"We'll come back after dark, when we're sure they're done cleaning," Henry said.

Jessie tried not to think about the cemetery at dark. She glanced back over her shoulder as they walked toward the stagecoach. Mrs. Caruthers was still standing there, watching them.

It made sense. She was a busybody. She was probably curious about how she could tell the town one of the Thompson brothers was escorting her around a cemetery. She wanted to find it amusing, but…

"I don't trust that woman," she muttered.

"Mrs. Caruthers?"

"Yes, it's probably silly, but she's always given me a gut bad feeling." She climbed into the coach and Henry did the same.

"We'll have Landon look into her. Never dismiss a gut feeling, Jess. Never."

THEY RETURNED TO the ranch. Cal decided to stay in town with Quinn at least until nightfall on the off chance the truck casing the apartment went by again.

They related what they'd seen, asked Landon to add Mrs. Caruthers to his list of people to look into, ate, then napped.

When they woke, they played a card game with Sara-beth and listened to her relate stories of Henrietta's antics.

It almost felt like a normal day for Henry, except instead of his usual hiding at the fringes, or grumbling at the fringes, he was in the middle of it all. Laughing with Sarabeth and Jessie like they were some kind of...

Well, it didn't do to think about.

They waited for nightfall. Henry wanted to find a way to convince Jessie to stay behind, but he knew it was likely a losing battle. He wasn't about to broach the topic unless he knew he had a foolproof argument.

Night was quickly falling and no such luck. Still, Landon talked with them a little about what he'd found.

"I looked into this Edith Caruthers. I didn't really find anything to raise suspicion, at least on the basics. One thing I did think was a little...weird, let's say, is her maiden name is Chinelly."

Jessie looked blankly at Landon. "Does that mean something?"

"It might not, but Rob had a connection to a guy named Ham Chinelly. A guy who helped him out when he was trying to get information from Hazeleigh. They were related by marriage, I believe."

"Well, I don't like that."

"Edith and Ham aren't siblings. I haven't found the actual familial connection besides the name, but it's not a common one. And in a small town like Wilde, it seems unlikely there's *no* connection."

"A connection to one person involved doesn't necessarily mean anything," Jessie replied. "I'm pretty sure half the town has some connection to a Peterson."

"But not Rob," Henry pointed out.

"Cal says still no sign of whoever Hazeleigh saw," Landon continued. "I don't like that, either. They might be laying low because they know someone caught on. Or they might be laying low because they have something planned. But they're laying low, one way or another."

Henry took that as his chance. He pinned Jessie with a serious look. "You could stay here with Sarabeth. You don't need to put yourself directly in harm's way."

"Neither do you," she said stubbornly.

"I don't have a kid counting on me, Jess."

She sighed. "I know. I know. But sitting here waiting?" She looked up at Landon, then back at Henry. "It doesn't make sense. I know too much. If you have trouble opening up the compartment on the stone, if you find something odd. I can make too many connections based on what might be on that map—if it's even *the* map. It makes the most sense for me to go."

"I could argue that," Henry returned darkly.

"You could, and I could argue that I don't need you, but you asked me to let you protect us, Henry. That's what I'm doing."

Henry didn't look at Landon, though he felt considering eyes on him from that direction. Still, he focused on Jessie. There was no good way to talk her out of this, so he had to protect her.

"We'll take my truck. We'll park at the back of the cemetery again. Avoid lights as much as we can. We'll get the map from the gravestone," Henry said. If he outlined the plan enough times, hopefully nothing went wrong. "We'll alert everyone we've got it. We'll head directly back to the ranch."

"Should Quinn and Cal stay at my apartment?"

"I'm thinking so. Just in case they see someone. Something." He looked up at Landon for agreement. And got it.

"And if Quinn acts squirrelly, Cal can warn us all," Henry continued.

"Maybe we should put one more person on the apartment," Landon suggested. "Without Quinn necessarily knowing."

"I like it. Dunne?"

Landon nodded. "I'll talk to him."

Landon went off to do just that and Henry went over the plan a few more times with Jessie. She went to put Sarabeth to bed and Henry stood on the back porch watching the sun fully set.

Landon came to stand next to him. "Dunne's on his way out. Cal and Quinn will stay put till he gets the signal."

Henry nodded, staring at the last glowing beams of light to the west. "Someone needs to be on any possible exit here. I don't think Sarabeth will run again, but that girl has a mind of her own."

"That she does. Weird owing your life to an eleven-year-old."

Henry slid a glance at Landon. He didn't seem bothered by it, exactly. Henry supposed it was just a kind of weird weight of feeling like you owed somebody. "Yeah, well."

Landon turned and grinned at him, waggled his eyebrows. "You're crazy about the both of them."

No point in arguing. It'd just prove Landon's point. So Henry grunted and looked back out at the fading sun.

"Nothing wrong with that, you know."

Henry couldn't help the bitter laugh. "Sure."

"I get the kid might be a complication."

"Sarabeth isn't a complication," Henry said firmly, and he knew it gave away too much, but it was just flat-out wrong to call her that. "And we don't need to have this conversation."

"I think we do," Landon said good-naturedly. "The thing is we all joined the military, and then Team Breaker, because we came from something that made us want to be more, right? Do something. Mean something. We wanted to prove it—to ourselves, and I imagine some of us to the people we came from. That we weren't as worthless as they made us feel."

"I didn't sign up to be psychoanalyzed by you, Landon."

"No," Landon said, clapping him on the shoulder. "You didn't even sign up to be my brother and a cowboy, but here you are. Because life isn't about signing up. The military was. But life isn't."

"That supposed to mean something?"

"Nothing wrong with letting the soldier go, the messed up kid go, and build a life—a real life."

"Well, that's all well and good for you and Hazeleigh." Henry could have been his normal mean and nasty self if he wanted to, but the words stuck in his throat. "Looks good on you."

Landon grinned. "Yeah. I imagine it does. Feels good. But you know, I was here for the great Jake and Brody fall too, so I know what it's like to look at it from the outside and think they must be built a little different. That somehow they're ready or good at it and you just wouldn't be."

"Trust me."

Landon shook his head. "But that's the thing. It's not magic or miracles or personality. Hazeleigh and I have our problems. Our hang-ups. Neither of us came from anything too great. But we decided to deal with them, work through them. Be honest about them. It's not rocket science. It's just…making a decision and sticking to it. You've always been damn good at that, Henry. Don't know why making a family would be any different."

"Families suck."

"The ones we were given? Sure. But the ones we choose?" Landon gestured at the ranch around them. "Not so much."

Choose seemed to be the operative word in this annoying little conversation. Chosen family. Choose to stick. *Choose, choose, choose.* "What about when you can't make the right one?" he managed to say, though he didn't care for the way his voice sounded rough and far too affected.

Landon took a moment. When he spoke, his voice was equally grave. "When push comes to shove, Henry, you tend to make the right ones. I know you wish you could have saved your mom. Or stopped that bomb back in that village, or been quick enough to get to the suicide bomber before Jefferson. I know what events haunt you, but those weren't choices, were they? Because if you'd had the choice, you'd likely have done it. And been dead in the process. So consider me one of the many who are glad you didn't *have* the choice in those scenarios."

Henry frowned at that. It made a strange, twisted kind of sense. He'd always blamed himself for not being able to stop his father but… If he waded through the emotions of that time, the pain of it, he could almost accept the truth that all the years he'd thought he should have done something, saved his mother in some way, the fact of the matter was he'd been eight. He'd been asleep in his bed. There was no way, at that age, at that time, he'd have been able to change the course of what happened.

No matter how much he wanted to. If there'd been a choice, he'd have made it. Maybe that was the true thing that had always haunted him.

No matter how much he wanted to save people, to make things right, sometimes the world just…didn't let you.

"Uh, well, howdy, Jessie," Landon said.

Henry didn't turn. He merely stood where he was and tried not to wince.

"I'm just…going to go do some more computer work."

Silence stretched out after Landon escaped inside and Henry figured it was cowardly to pretend like she wasn't there. Particularly when they had things to do. He turned slowly. Jessie stood at the threshold, hands clasped together. The porch light illuminated her face, but he couldn't read her expression.

But his heart kicked in his chest, something strange and foreign twisting deep in his gut. She was just… beautiful. And stronger than he'd given her credit for. A good mother, even with everything life had dealt her.

All those choices she hadn't had, but she had to face anyway because she wanted her daughter to be safe.

Henry would do anything, *anything*, to keep them both safe.

"I guess I should apologize," she said finally after the silence had stretched on too long.

"For what?" he muttered.

Jessie hesitated. "I listened to more of that than I should have without announcing my presence."

Henry didn't know what to say to that. He could hardly interrogate her on what parts she'd heard. Besides, he might have been vague, but she knew the stuff about his mother. Knew he'd been in the military. She knew…things he'd sworn no one would ever know outside his brothers.

He should be more…something. But it just didn't settle like he'd thought it would. It felt more like a relief.

He didn't have to say it himself. He didn't have to put her off himself. Now she knew and she'd—

She crossed the space between them, dark eyes never leaving his. He was afraid to read the emotion in them, but he couldn't seem to come up with the words to stop…whatever this was.

Because she didn't stop. She came right up to him, looked up at him and brought her hands up to his cheeks and held him there. Gently. Then she pressed her mouth to his.

Nothing could have undone him more, as he wasn't sure anyone in his entire life had treated him with gentleness. Certainly not a gentleness with this undercurrent of care. It should have scared him. Brought back that old anger as a wall against all the things fighting for purchase inside him.

But he only sank into it, felt somehow washed new.

She eased back and blew out a long, shaky breath, but when she opened her eyes, they were clear. Certain. "Let's go end this."

Henry didn't have any words, not after that, so he simply nodded.

Chapter Seventeen

They didn't speak the entire ride to the cemetery. Jessie didn't mind. It helped her work through exactly what had happened. What she felt.

And if she thought about the kiss, and the way Henry Thompson of all people had softened around her, she didn't have to think about gravestones and maps.

At least for a little while.

Henry slowed to a stop about the same place they'd parked the stagecoach earlier in the day. He pulled the keys out of the ignition, then handed them to her. "If you need to run, run."

"Henry—"

"No arguments. That's the rule. If you need to run, you trust me to take care of myself. I've survived war zones, Jessie. And I know you've survived on your own, but if there's trouble, I want you to get back to Sarabeth. That's all that matters."

Sarabeth was her primary worry. The number one on the list of what mattered. But she was hardly the only thing on that list.

"You matter. To me. To her. To your brothers."

"I don't plan on sacrificing myself," he said gruffly.

She understood what he was very carefully *not* saying. "But you would if you had to."

He sat there, staring straight ahead, but after a few moments of silence he finally turned to face her. "I would. That's just…who I am. I can't change it. I'd need to. I'd need you to let me."

She swallowed, because it wasn't just his normal fierceness, but a plea in his eyes. For her to understand. This wasn't about being noble for the sake of it. Protecting her because she couldn't protect herself.

It was simply who he was. Who he'd made himself out to be. Landon had spoken to Henry about choices, and Jessie knew from being a mother that some choices didn't feel like choices. "Okay," she managed, though her throat was tight with emotion. She took the keys he'd pressed into her palm.

If they ran into trouble, she'd run. To get help. To get backup. Henry had said it himself. Running could be okay. Fighting could be okay. She'd do whatever the situation warranted.

They got out of the truck. It was summer, but it felt a bit like Halloween with wispy clouds shading the moon, a cool breeze and hint of rain in the air.

She moved around to the front of the truck and Henry took her hand. Firm. Sure.

"Lead the way," he said.

She moved forward. It was dark, but the path was right here. There could be little ruts in it, but they should be able to follow it even in the dark. Henry had a flashlight in his pocket if they needed it, but they'd both agreed to do without light as much as they could.

"We're not going to run into any trouble," she said firmly.

"Way to jinx it," Henry muttered.

"You don't honestly believe in jinxes."

"I believe in all manner of things. Because I've seen all manner of unexplainable things."

"Don't tell me you believe in ghosts."

"Okay, I won't tell you."

Jessie was honestly shocked a man as…grumpy and cynical and smart and capable as Henry could believe in ghosts. She didn't.

Or hadn't, until she'd been walking through a cemetery in the dark with a man who did. The air twisted around them like it was spirits, not weather. Shadows flickered, moved, morphed.

She leaned into Henry and gripped his hand harder.

"Don't tell me *you* believe in ghosts," he whispered with just a hint of humor.

"Your fault," she muttered. They followed the path up the hill, then back down. She'd need a little light now, just to be sure she had the right stone. "You have the penlight?"

Henry handed it to her. She flicked it on and noted the gravestone in front of them, then thought about all the times she'd visited with Grandma. Then the one time after Grandma had passed.

"A few more to the left, then into the rows."

They moved. She turned on the light again to get her bearings, then hid it when she thought she could move without illumination. When she finally shone it on the obelisk that was her grandparents' grave, she let out a breath that was all nerves. To the right were her great-grandparents, and the monument with a removable nameplate where hopefully her grandmother's belongings still lay.

She moved over, ran her hands over the cold stone and didn't think about what lay beneath her feet. She handed the penlight to Henry. "Here. Hold it pointed right…there."

He did as he was instructed and she tried to undo the bolts. Age or disuse had fused them and she could no longer do it with simply her fingers. Brody had been the one who'd pointed out the possibility, so they'd thought to bring tools, thank goodness.

But it added time to the whole process, and it made nerves kick in. Henry pulled a little wrench out of his pocket and Jessie had to work in the small, dim light of the penlight to adjust it to fit the bolts on the nameplate.

It was still difficult to get the bolts to turn, especially when her fingers felt nerveless and fumbled.

She finally succeeded and let out a breath of relief. She tried to hurry, but Henry's free hand patted her shoulder.

"Take it easy. Take a breath. We've got time."

Time. *Time*. Why did that make her want to laugh? What *time* did they have? She'd lived under this shadow ever since she'd turned thirteen and now all she wanted wasn't time, but a conclusion.

Still, she took a breath so she didn't drop the bolt when it finally came loose. She worked methodically on the other three bolts. By the time she got them all off, she was breathing hard.

She handed the wrench and bolts to Henry so she could use both hands to pull the plaque off the stone. She had to get her nails in there and really wiggle it to get it to come off. The sound the metal made against the stone creaked loudly in the quiet night.

But Jessie couldn't think about that. Henry shone the light into the little crevice. Everything she'd put there when she'd been just a little older than Sarabeth was still in place. The pearl necklace, her grandmother's wedding rings, the little diary and…the rolled up map.

Swallowing against an odd swell of nerves, Jessie reached in and pulled the map out. For now she'd leave the rest. Come back when she knew… When she knew everything would be safe.

In fraught silence, she began to replace the plaque, map secured under her arm. But curiosity got the better of her and she didn't bother to tighten the bolts. She took the map and began to unroll the paper, to examine if it really was some kind of treasure map, but the penlight clicked off. Before she could protest, Henry's arm came around her shoulders, holding her still.

"Shh," he murmured.

She fell silent and stood as still as her racing heart would let her. Henry slid the paper from her fingers. Nerves jangled, but Jessie managed to breathe in time with Henry rather than hyperventilate.

Someone had to be here. Jessie closed her eyes, focused not on the possibility of danger but on the fact she was here with Henry. They would work together to avoid the danger.

She felt the slide of something against her back pocket and realized Henry was slipping the map into her pocket. Out of sight.

Part of her wondered if they shouldn't just give up the map. Hand it over and run. Let whoever find the damn treasure and leave them out of it. But she supposed that didn't really make them safe. Knowing about it made them probably as much of a target as anyone.

"We're going to move for the truck in the dark. Hold on to me. Step where I step. No light. No noise. Just move," Henry said, his voice barely a whisper. Barely anything above the whir of summer insects and nocturnal wildlife all around.

She didn't speak—she knew she wouldn't be able to keep her voice that even and quiet. So she nodded against his shoulder.

He took her hand and began to lead her forward. She trusted his lead. But she stopped and turned when she heard someth—

Pain exploded across her skull and she cried out. So surprised by it, confused by it, she didn't think. Simply let go of Henry's hand to fight off whoever had grabbed her by the hair. But in the dark she couldn't make out the shadow she was grappling with, and every punch or kick seemed to meet with air until a strong arm banded around her, keeping her almost completely still.

She wriggled, she fought, but it was no use. Someone had her.

A light appeared. Henry's. Not the tiny penlight,

but a stronger flashlight that nearly blinded her. She blinked against it when she heard Henry's voice cut through the quiet.

"I'd let her go if I were you," he said, low and dangerous.

"I'd give me the map if I were you." The hand in her hair tightened and she tried not to react, but then she felt something at her throat. Her knees wobbled. A knife.

Nothing on Henry's face changed, but everything about him was still. So still. It scared her almost as much as the knife at her throat, and the fact she recognized the voice.

Her father.

Henry's gaze flicked from the man holding her to her. Something in his expression flashed in all that stillness, but she wasn't quite sure what it was.

"I've got the map," Henry said. Which Jessie knew wasn't true. She was tempted to say that, so Henry would be left alone. But he'd asked her to let him protect her and she knew this was his version of that.

She also knew if her father knew she had the map he'd likely take it and slit her throat without a second thought.

"Let me go and he'll give it to you," Jessie said, managing to keep her voice even. She looked pointedly at Henry. *"Dad."*

Henry gave an almost imperceptible nod. "Remember what I told you in the truck?" he asked as if her father wasn't there, holding a knife to her throat.

Her mind raced with everything they'd said in the truck. He'd given her the keys. He wanted her to run.

"Shut up and hand over the map," her father said and she felt the knife dig a little into her skin. A sharp slice of pain.

But she couldn't let Henry know that. She had to be calm. She had to handle this. "I remember," she managed to say.

Henry nodded once, and then there was a blur of movement and her father's knife clattered to the ground.

When Henry told her to run, she did.

HENRY HAD NO doubt he could take down one lone knife-wielding man. The problem wasn't that. It wasn't even getting Jessie free without a scratch. He knew how to handle all of that easily enough.

It was the fact he doubted very much the man was truly alone. Which meant he'd just sent Jessie to run… possibly into someone else's clutches.

He didn't let himself dwell on that. There were immediate threats and *what-if* threats and thinking about *what-if* threats was likely to get a person killed by the immediate ones.

He'd had to drop the flashlight and though it was still on it was pointed in the opposite direction, so he fought the man—Jessie's *father*—in the dark. He dodged the knife the man had picked back up out of instinct and feel rather than being able to see it swinging toward him.

He landed an elbow to the gut that had the man doubling over, but Henry stumbled over a flat gravestone he hadn't seen and didn't manage to land the follow-up blow. He jumped back. The man's knife scraped against his jaw, but the cut would be shallow at best.

Unfortunately, the jerk away had him stumbling over another damn stone. A good reason not to have a fight in a cemetery, Henry thought wryly as he landed hard on his back against another stone.

He didn't groan in pain, but *damn*, that hurt.

The attacker stepped over the stone he'd tripped on. He was nothing but an approaching shadow, but Henry took the moment to catch his breath. The guy clearly didn't have a gun, so he had time.

"Don't know what you're getting yourself into," the man said, looming over Henry.

"And neither do you." Henry managed a kick that sent the man flying and gave Henry the precious seconds needed to get back to his feet.

Henry charged the man, but the attacker used gravestones as a kind of morbid obstacle course. Still, Henry knew he couldn't let him get away. This was Jessie's father. The ringleader. He had to bring him down.

Just as he managed to get a grip on the man, a gunshot rang out, loud and fatal against the quiet night, but Henry didn't feel the expected burn of bullet exploding through flesh—he knew just what that felt like. The man he was grappling with jerked, stumbled, fell.

Henry grabbed the flashlight, keeping low and behind gravestones as best he could. He pointed the beam at the man. He'd been shot in the stomach. It was a bad spot, but it wouldn't necessarily kill him if he got quick enough medical care. Henry scanned the area. Based on where they'd been, where the wound was, he had to assume the shooter was to the northeast. Maybe behind the big tree there.

There was no way to get to the shot man without exposing himself. He texted his brothers to pass the information on to an ambulance, the cops if need be. Jessie was out there somewhere running. Hopefully, she'd gotten in the truck and driven away, but unless he'd been too busy fighting to hear the sound, he'd heard no engines turn over.

Frustrated at the lack of options, Henry got as low as he could. No more gunshots rang out, but he didn't let that put him at ease. Carefully and quickly, he reached out an arm and began to drag Jessie's dad toward him. Where there'd be cover.

Another gunshot echoed through the night, but the sound of stone exploding wasn't as close as it had been.

"Not one of mine." The man laughed, actually laughed, as the blood spurted from his stomach.

Henry shrugged off his jacket and stripped off his sweatshirt. He rolled it up, pressed it against the man's wound. Then worked to get his coat back on, switching arms to keep pressure on the wound.

Sirens sounded far off, but they'd get here soon enough. Henry just had to keep himself from getting shot, too.

The man just kept laughing, even as he writhed in pain. "The ghost is going to get you. The ghost gets everyone eventually. Even me."

"I don't believe in ghosts," Henry lied.

"You're going to believe in this one."

Chapter Eighteen

Jessie didn't run to the truck. It would have been faster, sure, but if her father was out here, he wasn't alone. He never worked alone. Not ever. Which meant he had men out here, and likely had someone stationed at the truck.

How had he known about the map? The cemetery? Was he following them?

She had a hard time believing Henry had missed that, but maybe she was giving him far too much credit.

Except he'd handled that back there. Gotten her out of knifepoint, all so she could escape with this ridiculous map. She had half a mind to burn it and watch them all go insane.

But that was stupid. If she could get to the cops, she could hand over the map. Maybe they still wouldn't believe her, but she'd have evidence. They'd have to look into it.

And if they didn't, wouldn't, well, then she'd know she had to get back to Sarabeth and leave. Get out of here, off the grid again. It wasn't the childhood she wanted for her daughter, but alive was better than dead. Alive and on their own, even off the grid, was better than living in that compound.

Once she got far enough away, safe enough to risk the light of her phone, she'd text Cal and have him come help Henry. Text all of them to help Henry.

She had to believe Henry could hold his own until she was in a safer spot. He'd want her in a safer spot.

A loud *pop* echoed out across the night. Jessie had been running and breathing hard enough she could almost convince herself it was…nothing. Something else. Surely not…a gunshot.

She slowed, willed her breathing to even so she could listen. She got out her phone. She wasn't about to risk Henry this way. If it gave her away, so be it. She typed in a quick text to Cal.

Father at cemetery. I ran. Henry there. Have map. Help. ASAP.

She hit Send and then she heard it again.
Pop.
A gunshot.

She fought back her first instinct—to run toward it. Her father hadn't had a gun. If he had, he would have held that to her head rather than a knife to her neck. Had Henry brought a gun? She hadn't thought to ask. Not when they'd just been going to the cemetery to retrieve the map.

What now? She could run for the truck, for town, for safety. Or she could run back and make sure Henry was okay.

Henry wanted to protect her. Not because she needed it, but because he needed to do that. She understood—how could a mother not? Love was a complex motivator.

Love. Boy, did she not have time for that thought.

Another gunshot rang out and she flinched and crouched, as if that would somehow make a bullet miss her. But who could be shooting? There was no light. Only darkness. Even the wispy clouds had strengthened and covered the moon.

If someone was shooting it was either close range, or…

She swallowed. Well, she'd find out. Because she couldn't leave Henry here without access to the truck.

She pulled out the knife Henry had given her. It wouldn't save her from a gunshot, but if one of her father's men jumped out and grabbed her she could try to fight them off.

She thought of her own father holding a knife to her throat. So consumed by all this. It didn't make any sense.

No more gunshots rang out so she gave herself a moment to breathe, to orient herself, and to really decide if she wanted to go for truck or gravestone.

She thought she heard something… Not a footstep. Not a whisper. She wasn't sure what it was. Almost like a squeak.

Away from it or toward it? Shadows moved around her, but were they real? Were they friend or enemy? Was Henry still in there? Was he okay? She'd have to get to the other side of the cemetery to make sure.

She couldn't look at her phone now. Not when the light could draw unwanted attention.

She'd just get to the truck. Once she got into the truck...

Well, she'd turn it on. And if there was someone out there shooting, she'd drive away. If there wasn't, she'd wait for Henry to come.

She stepped forward, being careful to make a straight shot walking. When she thought she should be getting close to the truck, taking careful steps to test the ground, her foot nudged against something solid.

Warm.

Something—no, someone groaned. Jessie jumped back out of instinct. She couldn't make out what exactly was on the ground, but clearly it was a person. And though she'd never heard Henry groan, she didn't think it was him. The pitch was too...high. The body she'd accidentally nudged with her foot too soft.

Maybe it was whoever her father had assigned to watch the truck. Maybe Henry had gone through and disabled the entire group. He was capable. She was sure he was capable of that kind of thing.

But she had to be sure. Swallowing, she crouched and carefully pulled her phone out of her pocket. She hid the light with her body as much as she could, and leaned closer to the man on the ground.

Blond hair. Not Henry. Eyes closed. Pale face. Very bloody arm. And leg.

Jessie was rendered frozen for a moment. She didn't know what to do with someone hurt this way.

She looked at the screen of her phone. Cal had responded to her text. Nothing informative. Just: ok.

Jessie heard a noise and hurriedly shoved her phone

into her pocket. But another light popped on, along with the creaking sound of a door opening. The interior light on the truck. Her own face was outlined by the dim light.

No, not her face. Not *her*.

"Quinn." Jessie knew she should be scared. Terrified, really, but she was...hurt.

Quinn wasn't here to help. Not with a gun in her hand. Not looking at her like *that*.

Jessie's heart sank, and no matter how soft and silly it was, she felt...heartbroken. Quinn had never had a chance. Jessie had been given her—*their*—grandmother. A sense of normalcy before it had all been taken away.

Quinn had only had that compound and lies. So even with Quinn holding the gun, even knowing she might shoot, Jessie simply felt sorry for her. For them.

"Do you have the map?" Quinn asked. Her voice was very...blank. None of that bravado or pointed laziness. It was like she was a completely different person than she'd been the past few days.

And Jessie understood, as much as she didn't want to, that this was probably the real Quinn. Not funny and shocking and hard to read. Cold and calculating and here for the only thing everyone in her family cared about. Gold and treasure.

"Do you have the map, Jessie?" Quinn repeated. She didn't point the gun at Jessie, but Jessie was under no illusions she wouldn't use it on her if she saw fit.

She could lie. Just like she'd lied before. Tell her Henry had it. That would be the smart thing to do.

But her heart wouldn't let her. She took the map out

of her back pocket and held it up even as the sound of sirens could be heard in the distance. Maybe they'd get here fast enough. Maybe they wouldn't.

But there was no use pretending. "If this is really the map, I've got it."

THE SHOOTING HAD STOPPED. Henry could see the flashing lights now. He wasn't sure what had happened, and that sat all wrong.

There were clearly players in this he didn't know about. It couldn't just be Jessie's father and his goons, or why was the dad the one who'd gone alarmingly still and silent?

Henry could see the lights of the ambulance parked at the front entrance to the cemetery. He could wave them down, but he thought it'd be safer for them if he carried the unconscious man himself.

He supposed Jessie's father didn't deserve the courtesy, but life or death would be up to the hospital workers. Not him.

And should the man live to see tomorrow, Henry would make sure he paid for everything he'd done to hurt Jessie and Sarabeth. Dying was just a little too easy.

"You might wish you had died," Henry muttered, picking the man up. He groaned, moved a little and then went back to dead weight.

With the lights of the ambulance, Henry could make out the gravestones enough to avoid them as he carried the man to the medics who hopped out.

"Shot. Shooter is still out there as far as I know," he

said to the EMT who quickly worked to get a stretcher. Henry put the man down on it and the medics began to work.

They asked him questions, and cops arrived to ask him more. He answered them with enough information to make them aware of the dangerous situation they found themselves in, to maybe find the person shooting, or even Jessie.

But not enough to catch who he was or why he was here. He answered each question with an eye out to how to escape before they pinned him down or got a good look at him.

In the dark, in the confusion, with the skills he'd spent his adult life building, it was easy to slip away.

He started making his way toward the back of the cemetery and the truck. He didn't have the keys, but he was almost sure he hadn't heard it drive away. So Jessie was either waiting for him or...

It didn't do to think about the *or.*

As he reached the gate out the back side, he heard the telltale whistle from one of his brothers. He stopped, waited for them to materialize.

Cal appeared next to him.

"Where's Jessie?" Henry demanded.

"Not sure. Got a text all wasn't well, but she didn't say where she was and hasn't texted back. Listen—"

Henry swore. He had to get to Jessie before the gunman did. He started moving forward, toward where the truck was.

But Cal followed, and made it worse. "Quinn gave us the slip. Quite a while ago. She might be out here, too."

Henry stopped cold. "She got away from you guys?" He didn't have to see in the dark to know Cal's face would be cold fury.

"Used the bathroom window, climbed out the back. Dunne heard her, but he couldn't keep up with the leg. Apparently she can run like the devil."

"Apparently she *is* the devil," Henry growled. He reached the truck. It was unlocked, but there was no sign of anyone. He swore, viciously.

"Uh-oh," Dunne said. Apparently he'd been hiding in the shadows too, and Henry had been so focused on finding Jessie he hadn't noticed.

He needed to get his head on straight. For all of them.

"Got a man's body here," Dunne said. "Still breathing, but he might need one of those ambulances."

Another man shot. The bad guys, presumably. It didn't add up and they didn't have time to do a thorough search with the cops and medics crawling around.

He had to find Jessie before Quinn did. Before the gunman did.

Assuming they weren't one and the same.

Chapter Nineteen

"Give it to me, then," Quinn instructed.

She still didn't point the gun *at* Jessie, but it was right there and her finger was definitely on the trigger.

Jessie didn't care about the map in the grand scheme of things. She cared about the safety of her daughter. If she ran just to save the map and got shot, wasn't she just as bad as her family obsessed with this ridiculous "treasure"?

Jessie stepped forward slowly and carefully. Clearly, Quinn didn't *want* her dead, or she'd be shot already. Maybe if she went along with Quinn for a little bit, they could all get out of this in one piece.

Sirens were louder, their lights flashing not far off now. Were they coming here? Should she bolt?

"Quinn—"

"Don't say anything," Quinn hissed, grabbing the map and shoving it into her pocket as she scanned the world around them. She closed the truck door, but Jessie noted she did it soundlessly.

It was dark again. Jessie could run. Maybe she *should* make noise. Yell and scream.

Sirens were coming. If they were coming here because of her text to Cal, they'd go to the entrance likely. Not this back part. She should make a run for it.

Quinn's hand closed around her arm. "Not a word," she hissed. "Unless you want to end up dead."

Jessie swallowed at the nerves as Quinn grabbed her arm and dragged her through the cemetery, unerringly leading them around stones and fences and walkways.

Jessie didn't know how to handle Quinn, but she couldn't help but think she might be able to get through to her. Somehow. Maybe?

They were sisters. Identical *twins*. Even if they hadn't grown up together, even if Jessie hadn't known about her, surely there was some way to…to…something.

"Where are we going?"

"Shh! You want to die?"

It was strange the way she said that. Not like a threat. More like they were in this together. Though Quinn's grip on Jessie's arm was rough and authoritative as she pulled her along.

Jessie wondered if she pulled out of Quinn's grasp, would Quinn shoot her?

Quinn had led her out of the cemetery, in the opposite direction of the flashing lights.

"If you're taking me to our father—"

"You think our dad is the problem?" Quinn said, still in that hushed whisper. "You really don't pick up on anything, do you?"

Confused, Jessie pulled at her arm a little bit. Quinn heaved out a sigh and stopped. She brought her face close to Jessie's and spoke in a rushed, desperate whisper.

"Oh, he's mean and he's sneaky, but if he was half as smart as he thought he was, this would all be over. Instead, it's all family feuds and one-upmanship and... Look, I'll save you the details. You want to survive? Just follow me."

Maybe it was foolish to believe Quinn, to trust her. Maybe it was leading with an emotion the other woman didn't have.

But Jessie didn't have any better options. She didn't just *want* to survive. She needed to. For Sarabeth. For herself. For Henry even. She didn't want him heaping any more guilt on himself for things that were beyond his control.

So she let Quinn lead her deeper and deeper into the dark. She didn't say anything more. They moved through the evening shadows, quickly but cautiously. The sounds of whirring insects and the occasional hoot of an owl gave everything another echoing layer of tension.

Quinn stopped, pulling Jessie behind a tree with her. She didn't let go, but when she lifted the gun she pointed it outward. To the night around them.

"What about Cal and Dunne?"

"What about them?" Quinn returned irritably. Though she couldn't see in the dark, between shadow and the noise, she had the impression of Quinn turning her head toward her. "What? You think I shot them and left them for dead?"

Quinn sounded almost offended, which made very little sense to Jessie. But none of this did. "No. I just don't know how you got away from them. They're pretty..."

"Military guys are all the same. It's all *I know every-thing*. And *I'm big and strong and oh, so smart*. But you put on the waterworks, excuse yourself to the bathroom, they don't expect you to jump out of a window. Idiots."

Jessie blinked. "You…faked crying, and then jumped out my bathroom window?"

"More of a climb down than a jump." Quinn did her patented shrug. "Didn't count on Dunne being there, but I knew I could outrun him. A little surprised he didn't shoot, but eh. Maybe he's a bad shot."

"I can assure you, he's not."

"Whatever. Look, we need to be quiet again. I think I picked off most of what we have to worry about, but you never know. Follow me. Don't make a sound. Got it?"

It finally, fully dawned on Jessie what was happening. "You're helping me."

"What else would I be doing?"

Jessie didn't answer that. Didn't figure she needed to since Quinn knew very well what else she might be doing.

She let Quinn take her arm again, but then thought better of it. She pulled Quinn's hand off her arm and clasped it in her own. Just like Henry had done, leading her through the dark, hand in hand.

Then they moved. Through the dark. Quick, purposeful strides. Jessie worked hard to follow Quinn's every move so she didn't stumble. She got the sense Quinn was adjusting her pace to accommodate Jessie's slower strides.

Because she was *helping*.

This wasn't a mistake to trust her sister. They were

looking out for each other. They were going to get out of this together.

There was a noise, and then a splash of light that had Jessie flinching and squeezing her eyes shut. Quinn came up short, and Jessie bumped into her. But she kept her hand in Quinn's—both of them squeezing onto each other.

When Jessie could blink her eyes open, she realized Quinn had angled her body as if she was protecting Jessie from the light in front of them.

But Jessie could still see. She knew the man standing there with a powerful lamplight. Her heart sank. "Dad." If he was here, he'd somehow bested Henry. He'd somehow...

"No," Quinn said, and her voice was as flat as it had been back when she'd asked about the map. "I shot our father back in the cemetery," Quinn whispered. "Remember when I said George had a brother? Sadly, identical twins beget identical twins. That's our uncle. Gene. And now we're as good as dead."

THEY MOVED THROUGH the dark, a unit. Sticking to the shadows, avoiding cops and flashing lights. Cal thought he'd picked up a kind of trail at the truck, and Henry trusted him to catch the small cues.

He had to trust Cal, or the panic might overtake him completely. "Where would she have gone if not the truck?"

Cal came up short and looked around. They'd left the cemetery, and now that they were still, Henry realized they were far enough away not to hear the commotion of voices, see the flashes of lights.

Cal flicked on a flashlight. The beam was pointed at the ground. "Two sets of footprints," he said grimly.

Henry crouched to study them. "Awfully similar." It took an incredible force of will to sound calm when he posed his question. "You think Quinn got to her already?"

"Yes, but two sets of footprints moving means she's alive and well," Dunne offered.

"And being taken somewhere."

"Where? The father got shot."

"Maybe the father was the patsy all along and Quinn's the one who wants the treasure."

"She doesn't need Jessie for the treasure," Henry returned, and they began following the prints with Cal's light on. Slowly, quietly, so they could hear if they came up against something. "Jessie has the map."

"Maybe she didn't tell Quinn that."

"I think Quinn would have figured it out if she's behind this. If she's the mastermind."

"She's not," Dunne said. "She could have shot me."

"What?" Henry replied, turning to look back at Dunne before he remembered in the dark he wouldn't be able to make out Dunne's expression.

"She had a gun. I couldn't catch up, sure, but she could have shot me."

"Are you defending her?" Cal demanded.

"No, I'm pointing out there might be something else going on. That we need to be careful. Quinn might be in cahoots with the Peterson family nonsense, but we have to be careful not to make her out to be the only villain. She could have shot me, stopped me from telling you or anyone else what was wrong as quickly as I did."

"I'm pretty sure I would have heard the *gunshot*, Dunne."

"But I wouldn't have been able to tell you what happened."

"You could have shot *her*," Cal continued. Not willing to let the point go, clearly.

"I'm not about to shoot a scared, running woman. You really think we were *all* wrong and she's evil? Complicated? Sure. Evil? I don't see it."

"Maybe something's clouding your vision."

Dunne didn't respond in kind. He spoke calmly and completely unperturbed. "Or something's clouding yours. I'm suggesting we make sure to weigh all the facts rather than run off half-cocked. Something you're usually on board with."

Cal didn't have anything to say to that, and Henry didn't either, as they made their way through the dark night, following two women's footprints.

Not having a clue who to be on the lookout for.

SARABETH SAT CURLED up in the window seat in the living room. She knew the adults wanted her to go to sleep, but Mom and Henry were out there. She could lie in bed and stare at the ceiling, or she could sit here with Henrietta and watch for them to come back.

They had to come back.

Sarabeth sighed and leaned her forehead against the window. This was worse than last month. Just sitting here. Just waiting. Last month was scary, but she'd been able to do something about it. She'd had something to *do*.

She frowned a little at the dark outside. Something had…moved out there in the side yard. Her heart leaped to her throat. Mom?

But…no. Mom wouldn't lurk. She wouldn't hide. Neither would Henry.

Sarabeth scrambled from the window seat.

"What is it?" Hazeleigh asked from her spot on the couch where she'd been working on her laptop.

"I saw someone outside."

Hazeleigh set the laptop aside. "Okay, come on. Come here, away from the window." She held out her arms. "Landon?" she called.

"Someone is out there. This is bad. Someone…"

Landon came into the room, eyebrows drawn together. "What is it?"

"Sarabeth said she saw someone outside."

Landon frowned, but nodded. "All right. Let's—"

The window crashed and splintering glass went everywhere. Landon pushed her and Hazeleigh to the floor, covering them with his body.

Someone had shot it, Sarabeth realized. They shot the window where she'd just been sitting.

"They want me. They want to get me. I know they do." She tried to stand, but Hazeleigh held her in the corner. The rest of the adults were now in the living room, moving around. Jake and Brody had guns. Landon got to his feet.

"You stay here with Kate and Hazeleigh, okay?" he

said, not looking at her, but taking a gun from Jake. "Jake, Brody, Zara and I will take care of it."

"But they want me. They'll hurt you to get to me."

Landon crouched down in front of her, put his hand on her shoulder, just like Henry always did. He looked her right in the eye.

"What happened last month?"

"I... Well, I saved you."

"Exactly. Now it's our turn to save you."

Chapter Twenty

The man—Jessie's *uncle* apparently, another identical twin in this insane family who liked to keep them hidden away—demanded the guns and their phones and everything else. Jessie handed it all over, as did Quinn.

She did not hand over the map, and somehow, even when the uncle searched her pockets, he didn't come up with the piece of paper. When the man turned his head a little to talk to another man with him, Quinn sent Jessie a wink.

Jessie wished she could laugh or find some kind of comfort from that outrageous gesture, but some part of this would need to make sense. And it just flat out didn't.

"Get in."

Jessie didn't know what to make of *any* of this, but Quinn pulled her toward the car the man—her *uncle*—pointed at. Quinn all but pushed her into the back seat and then followed herself.

She leaned close to Jessie's ear. "Whatever you do, don't mention the map."

Jessie didn't have time to respond. The man got into the driver's seat. Another man got into the passenger seat. He pointed a gun at them. The uncle started to drive, no words exchanged.

She tried to get a handle on where they were driving. It was dark, but the headlights cut through the night. Gravel roads. Dirt roads.

Some started to look familiar. Or she was delirious. It was really hard to say. Closer to Wilde. Away from Wilde.

Why had she let Quinn push her into the car? They could go anywhere. They could be taken back to that compound, separated from Sarabeth. Henry could be…

But Quinn had shot their father, so Henry had to be okay, right? Somewhere out there, looking for her. Would he be able to find her?

The car pulled to a stop next to a truck. The driver got out, but the gunman stayed put. Still pointing the gun at them.

Quinn looked out the window, then turned to the gunman. She grinned at him, that languid laziness from the past few days back. "You can't honestly want to keep playing second fiddle to Gene."

The gunman rolled his eyes. "You can't honestly think I'd play second fiddle to *you*."

"I know something you don't," she returned in a singsong kind of voice.

The man narrowed his eyes. "We only need one of you, and I don't think it's you, Quinn."

Jessie's heart jumped at that. Quinn kept that antagonizing grin on her face, and Jessie realized… It was another form of protection. Quinn was trying to keep the attention, the threats on *her*. Not Jessie.

And Jessie just couldn't let her do it.

"But are you sure *she's* Quinn?" Jessie adopted the same pose of lazy disinterest. She cocked her head the same way Quinn did when she was trying to irritate people. "Seems like a gamble, bud."

He flicked a glance at Jessie, then at Quinn. Sneered. "It doesn't matter who's who. You'll both be disposable soon enough."

Jessie had to work very hard not to react to that. To keep a Quinn kind of facade above all her fear. They shouldn't have gotten in this car. They should just hand over the map and maybe…

Well, no, disposable meant dead. She wasn't that naive. Maybe there was no good way to deal. Maybe they were only going along until she had a chance to escape.

She'd thought that with Rob, too. And it had taken Landon, Hazeleigh and Sarabeth to make escape happen.

But she was alive. Sarabeth was alive and safe inside the Thompson ranch house far away. Even if the danger had come to that doorstep, Jessie knew everyone in that house would do everything they could to protect Sarabeth.

It filled her with a kind of strength. She would do everything to survive this for her daughter, but she also knew her daughter was in good hands.

Gene got back in the car and they began to drive again. It didn't take much longer for Jessie to recognize where they were going.

The Thompson Ranch.

Jessie's blood ran cold. "No."

Quinn reached over and gripped her hand, squeezing it. Reassuringly almost. Jessie tried to be reassured, but the car moved up the gravel drive and the house came into view.

Jake and Zara stood on the front porch, rifles pointed. Sarabeth, thank God, was nowhere to be seen. But she was here. In there.

They were here for Sarabeth.

The car came to a stop and the man with the gun pointed it at Jessie. "Get out."

"No," Jessie replied. He couldn't make her get out, and if he got out first, hopefully Jake or Zara would shoot first and ask questions later.

The man jerked the gun at her again. "I said get out."

"And I said *no*."

Her uncle sighed. Heavily. He pulled out a gun and reached back to point it directly at Quinn's forehead. "Get out of the car or I'll kill her in five, four, three—"

Quinn tried to hold on to her hand. "Don't listen to him—"

But Jessie pulled her hand free and scrambled out of the car. She had no doubt this could end in them both dead. If she got out of the car, she at least had a chance. She couldn't let Quinn die here.

Now she just had to find a way to get Quinn out of the car.

The passenger got out, the gun trained on her head the entire time. Quinn exited the car next, their uncle behind her.

Quinn and Jessie were human shields. But Jessie had

to trust the Thompson brothers and the women who'd helped her. And not just because Sarabeth had saved one of their own, but because it was…the right thing to do.

They wanted to do the right thing. The good thing.

"I suggest you lower those guns," Jake said from the porch. "It's not going to end well for you."

Her uncle laughed. "They'll both die before you even pull the trigger. Now, give us the girl."

HENRY WASN'T SURE how much longer he could bite back his frustration. The prints they'd followed ended at car tracks.

Cal pulled out his phone, checked on the texts and swore. "Landon says someone's at the house. Shot out the bay window."

Henry wanted to pound something to dust. Sarabeth was there, and though his brothers could handle any threat, he hated he wasn't there to handle it. "Quickest way there?"

Cal was consulting his phone. He pulled a face. "Cops back at the cemetery."

Henry swore. Again and again. "Wait. Either of you got the phone number for the one who's Zara and Hazeleigh's cousin?"

"I do," Cal said. Because of course he did.

"Was he up there?"

"I'm pretty sure I saw him," Dunne confirmed.

"Give him a call. Tell him to meet us at the highway. No sirens. No headlights if he can help it. I'm running."

Dunne took the phone from Cal. "You both run. I'll call."

Henry hesitated. You didn't leave a man behind.

But Dunne shook his head. "Go."

Henry didn't need a second urging. He took off west, knowing he'd meet the main highway that would take them out to the Thompson Ranch. Cal kept pace, but Henry doubted the same panic beat through him. The same blinding terror.

They made it to the highway, but there was no sign of the cop car. Henry wanted to scream in frustration, but instead, he took a deep breath and kept running. It wasn't as fast as a car, but he'd be damned if he was going to—

"There," Cal said, gripping his shoulder to slow him down.

Henry turned. No sirens. No lights—not even headlights, but the sound of an engine. It slowed and came to a stop. The passenger door popped open, the light illuminating Thomas Hart, Bent County Deputy, and Zara and Hazeleigh's cousin.

"Get in," he said.

Henry didn't need to be told twice. They both got into the car and Thomas took off, no lights, but plenty of speed.

"Thank God for cops who know the backroads, huh?" Cal offered.

"What's the situation?" Thomas replied.

Henry explained as best he could, best he knew. There were still a lot of question marks. But Thomas was able to fill in some.

"Someone picked off about four men in the cemetery.

No IDs on the men yet, but there was some chatter they were part of the Peterson family."

"You should talk to Edith Caruthers," Cal pointed out. "She might know something."

"Why? Because she's a busybody?"

"No," Henry returned. "Because I think she tipped off whoever it was that Jessie and I would be at the cemetery looking for something in the future. Slow down," Henry ordered as they approached the Thompson entry gate.

Thomas did as he was told, which moderately surprised Henry. "We should approach on foot. A surprise."

"Agreed," Cal returned.

"I'll radio someone to talk to Edith. Just give me a second."

"You can stay here and—"

"My cousins are here. This is my county. I'm a part of this. I'm law enforcement. I'm going in with you, whether you like it or not."

Henry didn't have time to argue with him. And besides, three was better than two.

"Okay. I'll come in straight ahead. Cal, you're west. Thomas, you're east once you radio it in. Meet at the house. The most important thing is whoever is shooting at the house they're after that little girl, and we're not going to let them lay a finger on her."

"What about the map?" Cal asked skeptically.

"Screw the damn map. Keep..." He stopped himself from specifying. For whatever reason. "Keep the civilians safe." Then he got out of the car and moved. He ran at first, keeping his footfall quiet against the gravel. He didn't think about Cal or Thomas. He focused on the target.

The front porch lights were on—he could tell that before anything else. He slowed his progress, made sure to be absolutely silent as he moved forward. He could hear the low murmur of voices, and paused behind a parked tractor.

He skirted around it, trying to get an idea of what was going on.

A car, not any of theirs, sat in the middle of the front yard with all its doors open. In front of it, two identical women being held at gunpoint by two men—one who looked oddly enough like George Peterson.

Jake and Zara were holding their own guns on the front porch. Henry didn't see anyone else, which meant Landon and Brody were likely guarding other exits, and Hazeleigh and Kate were keeping Sarabeth safe.

God, he hoped.

He couldn't tell which of the women was Jessie. Not in the dim light. Not when they stood still and didn't speak.

He supposed it didn't matter which one was Jessie. He needed to save them both, because he agreed with Dunne. Whatever Quinn might have done, it wasn't straight up evil, and she had a gun to her head at the moment.

The gunmen were using Quinn and Jessie as shields. They didn't expect anyone to come from the back. Henry wouldn't be able to pick them off with a shot— too close to the women, and he didn't have a quick enough gun to take them both out before the other might shoot the woman in front of him.

If he could communicate with Jake, they could do it in tandem, but Henry wasn't sure how he could do that without raising suspicion.

"Bring me the girl!" a man shouted. "I'm counting down and then they're both dead."

No, not on his watch.

"What about the map?" He heard Jessie say, and he finally knew which was which, because that statement was all Jessie. All about protecting her daughter. And the look Quinn sent her was *not* kind.

But it certainly got the attention of the man who was demanding Sarabeth.

"What map?"

Quinn sighed and reached into her shirt, pulling a folded piece of paper out of her, well, bra. "This one, geniuses."

But Henry couldn't watch what happened next. He saw something out of the corner of his eye. The flash of something. A shadow. Over by the stables. A small shadow.

Terror iced his veins. Was Sarabeth out here? No doubt she'd do something stupid to try and save her mother. Torn between the reality of Jessie being held at gunpoint and the potential of Sarabeth putting herself in danger, Henry didn't know who to go after.

Except, Jessie would never survive it if something happened to Sarabeth. She just…wouldn't.

He moved quickly through the shadows. Toward the stables. Toward the movement.

He stopped abruptly at an odd sound.

The *snick* of a match lighting. It illuminated the shadow. A *boy* held a match. Just a boy, but not one he recognized. He knelt down and...

Fire blazed suddenly, and the smell of gasoline burned his nostrils. He moved for the boy, but he realized the line of fire went straight for the stables. Where the horses were. Where Sarabeth's precious cats were.

Sarabeth.

He didn't know for a fact she was in there, but it would be a smart place to hide. Which meant Kate and Hazeleigh were likely in there, too. He ran for the door. Fire blazed in front of it, starting to lick up the sides, and with that illumination he could see that someone had tied the doors shut with a zip tie.

He heard Cal swear behind him. "What the hell."

"I think Sarabeth is in there."

Henry didn't have to say anything else. They moved as a team immediately. "I gave Jessie my knife."

Cal produced a small pocketknife and immediately began to saw at the plastic of the zip tie while Henry tried to beat back the flames with his coat.

"Gas," Cal said grimly.

Henry said nothing. He was about to yank the knife out of Cal's hands when the plastic finally fell to the ground. They each pulled a side of the door open, but a gust of wind sent the flames blazing higher and deeper into the stables.

"Sarabeth?"

"We're in here," he heard Hazeleigh say. She was very calm. Thank *God*. But there was nothing but fire.

No way to get to them. "The horses were already gone when we got here, then someone locked us in."

"I'll go around to the other side. Get an ax or something," Cal said.

"No, wait," Kate replied before he could dash off. "We soaked the horses' blankets in the drinking water. We can get across if we can get out on that side."

"Good. One of you come through with Sarabeth. Then Cal will help the other."

There was no discussion. Hazeleigh and Kate worked as a team, too. Wrapped in the sopping blankets, Kate and Sarabeth appeared. Sarabeth practically leaped for him.

"The bad men came for me," she said, crying into Henry's chest. "Where's Mom? Where's my mom? My arm hurts. I can't breathe."

Henry had to swallow against his own aching throat—not because of the smoke, but because she was hurt. He carried her with one arm, helped Kate with his other. Cal and Hazeleigh weren't far behind. They'd likely all have burns, smoke inhalation, so he had to get them outside. Away from the smoke.

Sarabeth cried into his shoulder. "I want my mom. I want my mom."

Once they were in fresh air, he squeezed her once, pressed a kiss to her hair and then handed her over to Cal. "Stay with Cal, baby. I'm going to go get her."

Chapter Twenty-One

Jessie could have hugged Quinn. It was clear Quinn didn't want to give up the map, but she was doing it. Jessie supposed she'd forced her into it, but Quinn didn't have to produce the map.

"That's not it," Gene said dismissively.

"Why don't you come find out?"

"I should have killed you when your father sent you," he said with a sneer.

"Yeah, you probably should have. Or one of you should have realized I don't have allegiance to either of you."

Jessie remembered what Quinn had said about where she'd gone when Jessie had arrived at the compound. She'd been vague. But she'd gone to live with the uncle. And likely was used as a pawn—her father trying to get information from the uncle, the uncle trying to trick their father.

"Only out for yourself, Quinn?" the other man said— the man who had a gun on Jessie.

"Shut up, Kirk. Daddy doesn't like mouthy little minions."

This Kirk guy lifted his hand like he was going to

try to hit Quinn, but Gene stopped him, and Jessie realized…he was his son. This was her cousin.

"Keep the gun on that one," Gene said, clearly disgusted with how easy it was to get a rise out of his son.

This was her family. Her uncle. Her cousin. Her identical sister. All brought to blows over some old gold.

"Hand it over," Gene said to Quinn.

With great reluctance, Quinn did. Jessie knew this wouldn't be it. It might keep their attention off Sarabeth, but it wouldn't *stop* anything. She glanced at Jake and Zara, still carefully holding guns. Like they were just waiting for their moment. Patient. Not risking anyone.

Then she saw…a shadow. Two shadows. Grappling. She could tell it wasn't Henry. A shade too tall, a shade too lean. But it was one of the Thompson brothers, grappling with another man.

It wasn't just Gene and Kirk. It was more.

Jessie swallowed at the grip of fear. She turned her gaze back to her uncle. Gene unfolded the paper, tilted it presumably to see it in the porch light. "Well. Look at you, Quinn. You might be useful after all."

Jessie didn't like this. She didn't… No, something bad was about to happen. They couldn't stand here being patient anymore. She had to act.

Gene nodded at his son. "Kill them."

Jessie lunged. She didn't think, just acted. She used the full force of her body to shove into Gene. It knocked him over, the gun clattering out of his hand before he could shoot.

And then it was chaos.

A gunshot. The thuds of bodies hitting the ground.

The new smell of smoke so acrid it made her eyes water, but she couldn't pay any attention to that. There was only keeping her uncle from shooting anyone.

She stayed on top of him. She couldn't see his gun, but she knew he likely still had it on him. She tried to pin his hands down, but one escaped and grabbed her by the throat, squeezing the breath from her. Still, she didn't get up. She used all her weight to keep him down, to keep him from bucking her off.

She couldn't risk looking around, seeing if she had help. She had to get the man's gun off him. But she couldn't breathe with his grip on her neck. She tried to pull away, but he was so strong. She wasn't winning anymore.

He was.

"I'm going to kill you, and then I'm going to take your daughter," her uncle said, though his breathing was labored as they struggled. "Not to kill her. No, that would be too easy. I'm going to make her mine in every way that counts."

The ball of fury was so big and so bright, it took over every rational thought. She couldn't breathe to scream, but a noise came from within her and she lunged forward, clawed his face. She used her elbows, her knees She paid attention to nothing but inflicting harm on this *evil* man who would dare threaten her daughter.

His grip on her neck loosened. He landed blows of his own, but she could barely feel them between gasping for air and biting, scratching, kneeing.

Until he stopped moving. Until there was only the

odd gurgling noise coming from his throat. She slowed her blows, saw the glint of his gun and reached for it.

"Jessie!" Quinn's voice. She looked toward it. Just as Kirk turned his gun on her.

She was going to die.

It was the only thought in her head as the gunshot rang out.

HENRY WAS ONE second too late.

But Quinn wasn't.

She stepped in front of Jessie and as the gun went off, she fell almost simultaneously as *another* gunshot rang out. The shooter jerked back, stumbled and fell to the ground.

Henry rushed forward, along with just about everyone. Jake and Zara from the porch, Thomas from wherever he'd been, Brody from the back.

Jessie knelt next to Quinn, while Jake barked out orders, making sure all men were disarmed and taken care of and everyone was accounted for.

But Henry could only move next to Jessie. "Jessie—"

Jessie was touching Quinn's face as Thomas was working to find a way to stave off the blood seeping from Quinn's leg.

"She saved me. I thought… I thought it was her, but then she helped and protected me and saved me."

"You're okay?"

Jessie nodded, her eyes on Quinn. "She has to be okay."

"She will be." God, he wished Dunne were here so he could know whether he was lying or not.

"Ambulance is on its way," Thomas said. "Sent a call out the minute I saw that fire go up. Cops will be here, too."

"Move aside."

Henry looked up to see Dunne stride through the chaos.

"Landon's bringing my supplies. You've got an ambulance on the way?"

Thomas nodded. "You a doctor?"

Dunne gave Henry a look. Henry knew exactly what it meant. Would they give more of themselves away here?

Henry nodded.

"Combat medic," Dunne answered. "I can get her stabilized while we wait."

"Is she going to be okay?" Jessie asked.

Dunne knelt next to Quinn's very still body. "We'll do everything we can, Jessie. Why don't you step out of the fray?"

Henry gently pulled her back. She resisted, but he knew what buttons to push. "Sarabeth wants you."

Jessie nodded. "She… Quinn stepped in front of a bullet for me."

"You're sisters."

Jessie shook her head and leaned into him as he led her to the house. "But…" She didn't seem to have anything to say about that. She seemed to realize… She took his hand. "You… You're burnt. What happened?" She looked around, gasped at the stables.

"Little fire. It'll be all right. No one was hurt too much. Come on now. Sarabeth—"

The little girl ran out the door and into her mother's

arms. They cried all over each other and Henry just…
stood there. Maybe he should give them privacy, but his
relief was too great. He just wanted them in his sight.
He wanted to…

Jessie reached out an arm. He took it and she pulled
him in. Like a three-person hug. Though they were hurt
and smoky and both women were still crying, they were
holding on to him. Bringing him into the fold.

So he wrapped his arms around them and indulged
in a breath of relief. They were safe. They were okay.

The sirens sounded, and lights flashed. The ambulance would get here and Quinn would be okay… It
would all be okay.

It had to be.

Over the next few hours, Quinn was taken to the
hospital. Everyone got checked out by a medic. Cops
took the injured men away. Landon, Brody and Cal
surveyed the fire damage, while Dunne lectured anyone with burns how to handle their wounds. Sarabeth
dozed in Jessie's lap in the living room, and Henry
knew that was the only thing keeping Jessie from racing to the hospital.

He'd take her there himself later, but Quinn was in
surgery and Jessie needed some rest herself. She already
had bruising on her throat, and her hands were scraped
and bandaged from attacking her uncle. It hurt Henry
just to look at her, but he also couldn't look away.

She was okay. Here. Okay. Both of them.

When Thomas entered with Landon and Brody, everyone quieted. And sat down in the living room. Henry
stopped pacing and settled in next to Jessie.

Thomas's face was as soot covered as the rest of them and he thanked Hazeleigh when she brought him a glass of water.

He cleared his throat, then with a look at the sleeping Sarabeth, spoke carefully and quietly. "Well, we've got a ways to go to work through the whole mess, but there are some things I can tell you. Edith Caruthers talked. She gave one of our deputies a list of names of those involved in this treasure map scheme, as she called it. She wasn't involved, she claims, but giving the names will help her case if it goes to trial. Four of the names matched the shooting victims at the cemetery. I imagine we'll find the same goes for the men we rounded up here, but we're still working on IDs."

"Is Gene still alive?" Jessie asked, her voice low and controlled. Henry knew in part to keep from waking Sarabeth, but in part because she didn't know how to feel about it.

"He is. You did quite a number on him, but he'll make it. We talked to the police in Idaho and both Gene and George are wanted on a lot of charges, so we've posted cops at the hospital to make sure there's no funny business. Idaho sounded like they'd bring the feds in, so it seems unlikely you'll have to worry about any of them once they've healed. They'll likely head straight to jail."

Jessie closed her eyes, and Henry could feel her absolute relief. But it was only for a moment or two. "Deputy Hart... What on earth do we do about this treasure?"

Thomas scratched a hand through his hair. "Well. I'm not sure. Old treasure isn't my area of expertise. We'll check on that and get back to you."

Jessie nodded and smiled wanly. "Thank you, Deputy Hart. Really."

He answered a few more questions, promised to be in touch and then he left. No one got up right away. Everyone just kind of sat there.

It was Jessie who finally broke the silence. "I can't begin to thank…" Her voice broke and she pressed fingertips to her eyes. She cleared her throat and tried again. "I am so sorr—"

"No," Henry said firmly. He would *not* let her apologize.

"Henry, I brought all of this on your doorste—"

"No," he repeated. "You needed help. We offered it. It was the right thing to do. I don't have any regrets."

"But…" She looked around at all the other faces in the room.

For the first time in a long time, Henry took stock of the people in his life. The men he trusted, who'd become his brothers. All who assured this woman that she wasn't to blame. That help was help.

He'd been a grumpy SOB for a few years now. Sarabeth had been right when she'd come to him. He was the mean one. It was a role he'd leaned into after their military careers had ended.

But he didn't want to be that anymore.

Epilogue

A month later

Sarabeth Peterson was eleven years old, but tomorrow she would be twelve. She was excited about her birthday, but she was more excited about today. Because she was finally, *finally*, going to be able to see the treasure.

Her treasure.

She knew Mom didn't like the idea that they owned the treasure—she and Aunt Quinn—but Sarabeth *loved* the idea, and now that all the people who needed to sort those things out had, and Aunt Quinn had come home from the hospital, they could go look.

No one had told her to call Quinn *Aunt*, but she was Mom's sister, so that made her Sarabeth's aunt.

Sarabeth was pretty sure Aunt Quinn was the only one who was as excited about the treasure as she was.

"Are we there yet?"

Henry looked at her in the rearview mirror. "Does it look like we're there yet, kid?"

She didn't like it when anyone called her *kid*. Except Henry. She liked it a lot when he said it. She liked it even more when he said it and then gave her mom a look afterward. It was kind of a...lovey look, she'd decided. Not that she'd tell them that.

Or that she watched those lovey looks closely, hoping it might mean they could stay at the ranch.

They hadn't had to go back to the apartment yet. Mom didn't want to live above Mrs. Caruthers, who'd gotten in some trouble but not enough to put her in jail. She also didn't want to live in a place with tall stairs because Aunt Quinn wasn't fully healed yet and Mom was determined to look after her.

So Henry had convinced her to stay at the ranch, but Mom was always saying how it wasn't permanent.

Sarabeth was going to see about that. The way she saw it, they *all* belonged at the ranch. Even Aunt Quinn. It worked. Everything was great.

Mom hadn't *thanked* her for asking Henry for help all those weeks ago, but the way Sarabeth saw it she probably should.

She sighed heavily and then looked over at Aunt Quinn. She still didn't look so good. Even Sarabeth could tell. But she kind of thought that was why Mom was even letting them go look at the treasure, to cheer Quinn up.

Henry pulled to a stop in front of a kind of...barn. Only it was round. And old-looking, but it had a lot of odd windows and rusty metal.

The nice police officer was there and he smiled warmly at all of them when they got out. "You all look a lot better than the last time I saw you."

"Where is it?" Sarabeth demanded.

When all the adults chuckled, she scowled. She *hated*

when adults laughed at her. Still, the police officer led them forward and undid a padlock and gestured them inside.

It was like a fairy tale. There were tables of things. Gold things and silver things. Jewelry and things Sarabeth didn't even know *what* they were.

"Jackpot," she heard Aunt Quinn whisper.

JESSIE LET SARABETH and Quinn move to look at everything. She…wanted nothing to do with it, truth be told.

"We worked with the feds and they confiscated some things that could be returned, but most of it's too old to go back to original owners," Thomas explained. "Since you're both on the deed for the land, it's technically all yours."

"Deed for the land," Jessie echoed. "I don't own any land here."

"Uh, that's not what the records say. They say you and Quinn were deeded it on your grandmother's passing."

"Grandmother…" She'd had the map. And the deed to the land. "But she wasn't a Peterson."

"That's a mystery I can't solve for you," Thomas said with a kind smile. His phone beeped and he looked at the readout. "Excuse me for a second."

He left the round barn. Jessie looked up at Henry. "It doesn't make sense."

"I'm sure you and Quinn will figure out a way to make it make sense. Besides, you're basically loaded now. You can hire a private investigator. You can do all sorts of things."

All sorts of things. Jessie frowned. At him. At the treasure. "I just have the terrible feeling this is all... cursed." Jessie watched Sarabeth bound around, Quinn hobbling behind her. They were both clearly so pleased, but Jessie couldn't get there.

"A woman who doesn't believe in ghosts can't believe in curses," Henry said, but he smiled at her.

She tried to keep a straight face, but couldn't manage. "And a man who believes in ghosts can't *not* believe in curses."

He grinned at her now. "Sure he can." She reached up and put her palm to his rough cheek. He grinned more and more now. Smiled. Laughed. *Enjoyed.*

She didn't care about this treasure. Hers was right here. With him. With Sarabeth. With her sister.

She had a family now. A real one she'd made.

Henry nuzzled into her palm. "I don't believe in curses, because we've both beat maybe not curses, but quite a few odds to stand here, alive and well. Take the treasure, Jess. You *survived.* You've got safety and a future now. To do whatever you want with."

She looked up at this man, who'd helped her simply because it had been the right thing to do. Who'd saved her daughter, time and time again. Who hadn't left her side as they'd sorted through weeks of aftermath.

He'd even brought her flowers.

He still scowled and grunted when the mood struck, but she knew he'd lightened up quite a bit. He laughed with Sarabeth, with his brothers. He...enjoyed the life and family around him.

It was still a strange concept that her life was her

own. All the old threats were gone and she well and truly could build a life for Sarabeth here in Wilde without fear. With her sister, her identical twin.

And with the man she loved.

"What about you?"

"What about me?"

"What do you want to do with your life?"

HENRY LOOKED DOWN at the woman who'd changed that life. He'd been through a lot of changes. Most of them bad. A few good.

She and her daughter were by far the best.

"I don't want you to leave the ranch."

"That's an *I don't want*, not an *I want*."

Henry grunted, his smile dying a little. "Fine, I want you and Sarabeth to stay."

"Why?"

He looked at her, really looked. Soaked it in. How lucky he'd gotten, after such a rotten start. Her, too, after a rotten middle. And here they were.

So no, he didn't believe in curses. He believed in something else entirely.

"Because I love you and your daughter. And I want to be with you and build a life with you."

"Well." She cleared her throat, leaned into him and furiously blinked back tears. "I guess it's lucky that's what I want, too."

He leaned his mouth to hers. "Why?"

She laughed, her eyes alight with amusement and emotion. "Because I love you, Henry. And Sarabeth loves you."

Because treasure didn't matter. Changes could be good and bad. Life was life, always plowing on, but you could choose to focus on the good over the bad, or as much as the bad. You could change the course of your life.

Because curses weren't real.

But love was.

* * * * *